DISENCHANTMENTS

An Anthology of Modern Fairy Tale Poetry

Published for University of Vermont
by University Press of New England
Hanover and London, 1985

DISENCHANTMENTS

An Anthology of Modern Fairy Tale Poetry

edited by WOLFGANG MIEDER

University Press of New England

Brandeis University
Brown University
Clark University
University of Connecticut
Dartmouth College
University of New Hampshire
University of Rhode Island
Tufts University
University of Vermont

Printed in the United States of America

Library of Congress Cataloging in Publication Data

Main entry under title:

Disenchantments: an anthology of modern fairy tale poetry.

Bibliography: p.

1. Fairy tales—Poetry. 2. English poetry—20th century. 3. American poetry—20th century. 4. Folklore—Poetry. 5. Grimm, Jacob, 1785–1863—Adaptations. 6. Grimm, Wilhelm, 1786–1859—Adaptations. I. Mieder, Wolfgang.

PR1195.F343D57 1985 821′.008′037 84–40592

ISBN 0–87451–327–8

Acknowledgments for use of previously published material and illustrations are listed beginning on page 197

CONTENTS

INTRODUCTION

A closer study of fairy tales would teach us what we can still expect from the world.

ELIAS CANETTI (1943)

Interest in fairy tales has increased tremendously in the last two decades. Beautifully illustrated editions of Grimms' tales in particular can be found in bookstores everywhere, and children's ongoing fascination with fairy tales is matched by the serious attention that scholars pay to them. Cultural and literary historians, sociologists, folklorists, psychologists, and others who have studied the deeper meanings of fairy tales all attest to the universality of these traditional narratives. Although they depict a supernatural world with its miraculous, magical, and numinous aspects, fairy tales present in a symbolic fashion common problems and concerns of humanity. They deal with all aspects of social life and human behavior: not only such rites of passage as birth, courtship, betrothal, marriage, old age, and death, but also episodes that are typical in most people's lives. The emotional range includes in part love, hate, distrust, joy, persecution, happiness, murder, rivalry, and friendship, and often the same tale deals with such phenomena in contrasting pairs, that is, good versus evil, success versus failure, benevolence versus malevolence, poverty versus wealth, fortune versus misfortune, victory versus defeat, compassion versus harshness, modesty versus indecency; in short, black versus white. What distinguishes all fairy tales from other oral or written narratives is, of course, that the conflicts are resolved in the end. Happiness, joy, contentment, and harmony become the optimistic expression of a world as it should be, where all good wishes are fulfilled.

Little wonder that such tales of a poeticized and perfect world have seemed appropriate literature for young and innocent children since the Victorian age. A child learns from them that certain problems, dangers, and ordeals may, if met with perseverance, be surmounted. Since fairy tales usually present a simple plot that proceeds from a negative state to a positive resolution, child psychologists have long argued that children will understand their symbolism to mean that transformations are necessary, that changes will and must take place, and that everything will work out in the end. Children will reinterpret their own lives and experiences according to the fairy tale messages, even though this process might go on subconsciously, and they will gain an optimistic and future-oriented world view of their own. They will learn to solve their conflicts imaginatively; ultimately, they will become independent and socially responsible people, and will reach a higher realm of being where the search for personal pleasure is replaced by a sound understanding of social reality. But these are utopian hopes and dreams of psychologists, for obviously fairy tales alone do not make a perfect human being. They can, however, help children as well as adults to understand universal human problems better, for at the level of a children's story or of adult literature, fairy tales provide a key to a better understanding of one's own being and the world at large.

There can be no doubt that traditional fairy tales are still told, read, heard on the radio, or seen on the television or movie screen, and that children continue to be enchanted by them. While for children they are absorbing and wonderful fantasies, it must not be forgotten that these narratives stem from earlier times and that they contain elements of social history for a time far removed from the present. Their morality and ethics do not necessarily correspond to the modern value system of a technological society. They often camouflaged the trials of oppressed people against unfair rulers, the conflict between the have-nots and the haves, the desires for a fairer political and social order, and so on. Behind the poetic symbolism of many fairy tales lies the gruesome reality of the Middle Ages from which the common folk escaped into the stories that we now know as fairy tales. In other words, the tales that have been read as beautiful and simple stories of luck, happiness and wish fulfillment by generations of children were in fact not invented for children. Only with the Brothers Grimm did these adult stories become the *Children- and Household Tales*

(*Kinder- und Hausmärchen*) that have influenced youth ever since. But the "sweet" and "cute" tales conceal the frustrations of adults of another age who longed for a better and fairer world, where good would win out over evil, and where in fact all people could live happily ever after.

It must not come as a surprise, therefore, that when rereading or remembering the fairy tales with which they became so well acquainted as children, adults often respond quite differently from the way psychologists predict. Once adults have lost their naive understanding of the fairy tale world, they tend to read fairy tales critically rather than symbolically. Having relinquished their dreams of a perfect world of happiness, love, and optimism, they question the positive value system of the fairy tales. Adults do not accept the positive solution of the old fairy tale any longer but, rather, are occupied with real-life problems. If unhappy and oppressed adults of earlier times formulated these tales as an escape from an ugly reality, modern people, who have often accepted a pessimistic world view at the expense of the optimistic view expressed in fairy tales, identify with the problems of former times that are also their own.

Thus it is of no consequence that Snow White, for example, finds her prince at the end and lives happily ever after. Much more interesting and "real" is her relationship with her stepmother (or evil mother), that is, the timeless mother-daughter conflict, or the sexual implications of her staying alone at the house with seven dwarfs who quickly, in modern interpretations, become transfigured into perverts.

It is the individual problems of the fairy tales that modern adults concentrate on, since these reflect today's social reality. After all, what normally intelligent person would possibly admit to believing in the optimism of the fairy tales? A good dose of negativism is inherent in our world view and probably rightfully. Although inside we may wish for a better existence, we are often preoccupied with problems that prevent us from finding that happy end. The positive vision of the fairy tales seems to become lost in a world riddled by pessimism, skepticism, and cynicism.

Yet modern mankind cannot and probably should not free itself from the traditional fairy tales. Luckily they are common knowledge, and as such are familiar to almost everybody, as only the Bible and a few other great written works are. Because they are part of our heritage, we can communicate with them and through them. Fairy tales are not only stories of enchantment for children but also a form of entertainment (humorous and serious) for adults who reinterpret them innovatively. Since modern interpreters of the tales often look critically at particular problems in individual fairy tales, the tales are seen as reflections of a troubled society, as a critical view of the belief in perfect love, as a concern with sexual matters and so on. The happy end of the old fairy tale is more often than not forgotten or negated. Such modern reinterpretations of fairy tales are most effective when contrasted with the traditional version, that is, when wishful thinking and reality are juxtaposed. The resulting interplay of tradition and innovation not only takes place in people's personal reactions to fairy tales but can also be seen in movies and on television, on records, in advertisements, in comic strips, and in cartoons. The popularity of fairy tales or at least individual fairy tale motifs in the mass media is increasing and speaks of the regeneration of fairy tales.

A questioning reaction to fairy tales became common in the middle of the nineteenth century. Such well-known classics as "Sleeping Beauty," "Little Red Riding Hood," and "Snow White" among others inspired poetic variations in the form of plays, operas, stories, and, above all, ballads and poems. At the beginning of this vogue these adaptations, especially those cast into lyrical forms, were usually more or less precise retellings of the tale. Such authors as Tom Hood, John Greenleaf Whittier, James N. Barker, Frances Sargent Osgood, Bret Harte, Samuel Rogers, and even Alfred Tennyson delighted in writing such poems. But by the turn of the century a tendency to confront the fairy tale world—through humor, irony, or satire—with a less favorable reality became discernible. Questions of guilt, deception, marriage, love, emancipation, and so on, began to be raised, changing some of these earlier fairy tale poems to anti-fairy tales.

Realistic reinterpretations of entire fairy tales or certain motifs have become the rule in modern fairy tale poetry, a subgenre of lyric poetry that has received little recognition from the scholarly world. Even though some literary historians have commented on the fairy tale poems by such poets as Randall Jarrell and Anne Sexton, the fact that many modern poets have written fascinating poems either based on fairy tales or at least alluding to them has been overlooked. At the beginning of this century James Whitcomb Riley composed a number of generally traditional fairy tale poems, and his "Maymie's Story of Red Riding Hood" was even written in dialect. But contrast such a poem with the recent retelling of several popular fairy tales for children and adults by Roald Dahl. In his lengthy poems the fairy tales are restated in the jargon of the modern world, so that one finds in his poems, for example, such words as "discos," "pistols," and "panty hose." Dahl has brought fairy tales up to date, somewhat as James Thurber did in his short prose texts.

A few poems still exist that contain somewhat positive reactions to the perfect world of the fairy tale endings. As an example, Joy Davidman's "Rapunzel" poem, "The Princess in the Ivory Tower," comes to mind; though even in this poem it is not clear whether the prince will reach his beloved or not. And the poem "Reading the Brothers Grimm to Jenny" by Lisel Mueller, clearly written by a mother for a child, also does not remain unproblematic, juxtaposing as it does the wonderful world of fairy tales and the dangerous world of reality. Only a few poems retain the peace and harmony reached in the conclusions of the original tales. Yet, with the exception of some humorous poems that are in fact ridiculous nonsense verses, the modern Anglo-American fairy tale poems are critical reactions to fairy tales that are no longer believed or accepted. Transformed into parodistic, satirical, or cynical anti-fairy tales, these poems often contain serious social criticisms. By reading these modern renderings the reader is supposed to reevaluate societal problems. The unexpressed hope is perhaps that such alienating anti-fairy tales might eventually be transformed again to real fairy tales in a better world. Many fairy tale poems are therefore deeply felt moral statements.

Modern fairy tale poems concern themselves with every imaginable human problem: there are poems about love and hate, war and politics, marriage and divorce, responsibility and criminality, and, of course, emancipation as well as sexual politics. Such productive fairy tale poets as Sara Henderson Hay, Anne Sexton, and Olga Broumas deal specifically with women's concerns and do not shy away from homosexual issues. Their poems are never vulgar or promiscuous—they are sincere personal expressions. The emotional intensity of these poems can perhaps best be expressed in the lyrical form and by means of fairy tale elements. Psychological investigations of fairy tales have shown that they can be interpreted sexually, and it is therefore not surprising to see modern renditions along these lines. But sex is only one major theme of these poems. Many of them also deal with such problems as greed, cruelty, deception, lovelessness, vanity, materialism, power, and irresponsibility. The adult world is simply not perfect any more. The philosophical fairy tale poems by Randall Jarrell especially capture the frustrations that modern mankind experiences in a world void of happy endings. But as was stated previously, many of the pessimistic statements conceal a quiet hope for a better world where these anti-fairy tales will once again become fairy tales. As Jarrell puts it at the end of his poem "The Märchen (Grimm's Tales)":

> It was not power that you lacked, but wishes.
> Had you not learned—have we not learned, from tales
> Neither of beasts nor kingdoms nor their Lord,
> But of our own hearts, the realm of death—
> Neither to rule nor die? to change, to change!

Changes are necessary in an increasingly complex world. Let us hope that such transformations lead humanity to positive solutions to its difficult problems.

In the present anthology 101 fairy tale poems by 78 authors of English-speaking countries have been assembled for the first time. This collection is the result of more than a decade's work, searching out these poems in books of poetry, poetry journals, and literary as well as cultural magazines. Only poems from this century have been included since poems of the nineteenth century are often lengthy and usually just retell the fairy tale plot in rhymed form. The more modern poems are often rhymed as well, but many of them appear in free verse, while others even adhere to the stricter form of the sonnet. The average length is about one printed page, and it is amazing how much of the original fairy tale together with a critical discussion of it can be stated in so few lines. Obviously the poems differ greatly in literary and intellectual value, but all of them are modern reactions to traditional tales and motifs. Satirical poems stand next to humorous or even silly or nonsensical ones, and an ironical text may follow a serious love poem. In the poems joy is followed by sorrow, happiness gives way to grief, and love is overtaken by pain, but laughter and hope as well as love and peace also have a place in these poems. Although the mood of each poem is different, together they represent the concerns of modern mankind expressed through a reaction to fairy tales of the past.

Usually I have included only one poem per author, but some—Robert Graves, James Whitcomb Riley, William Hathaway, Olga Broumas, Sara Henderson Hay, Randall Jarrell, Anne Sexton, and Roald Dahl—have two to nine texts. Anne Sexton with five and Sara Henderson Hay with nine poems in this anthology are also the most prolific fairy tale poets, each having published an entire volume of such poems. The poems in this collection are arranged into eleven chapters; the first two present a potpourri of poems that talk in general about the sense of fairy tales today and poems that react to various fairy tales or motifs. The remaining nine chapters deal with the most popular Grimm fairy tales, and they are arranged according to their sequence in the standard Grimm collection. "Sleeping Beauty" is clearly the fairy tale that today's poets react to most frequently, and this chapter includes twenty-three poems. This tale of love, beauty, and sleep is often reinterpreted along emancipatory and sexual lines, but this chapter also includes beautiful love poems as well as humorous texts. The chapter entitled "The Frog Prince" has thirteen poems; this story is popular in the adult world both because of its erotic implications and because of its symbolic message, namely, that promises must be kept. And there is "Cinderella," which contains fourteen poems; many deal with the female liberation from oppression. Similar views are expressed in some of the eight poems based on "Snow White." In every chapter the poems are arranged chronologically, and their dates of appearance, the dates of the authors, and bibliographical references are listed at the back.

Each chapter compiles several poets' reaction to a given fairy tale. Juxtaposed with one another, they clearly indicate that fairy tales deserve reflection today and in the future. Their universal nature demands reinterpretation.

These poems are meant for adults just as the original fairy tales were told among adults to help them cope with the hardships, worries, and uncertainties of everyday life. Collectively the poems acknowledge the fact that we do not live in a fairy tale land; and though we may laugh at the naiveté of the surface structure of fairy tales, they provide a vehicle for the expression of profound human feelings. Although we may be disenchanted with our troubled world and with traditional fairy tales, the innovative fairy tale poems assembled here may help change the world for the better. If so, the universal value system expressed in the deep structure of the fairy tales will have triumphed.

I would like to thank my colleagues and friends Professors Jack Zipes, David Scrase, and Frank de Caro as well as my students Trixie Stinebring, Clifford Timpson, and Antje Justice for providing me with some of the poems. I also wish to express my appreciation to Professor Henry Steffens, Dean John G. Jewett, and Vice President Robert Lawson from the University of Vermont for their continued support for and encouragement of my research projects in folk narratives. It gives me great pleasure to dedicate this book to my niece Nancy and my nephews Bradley, Clay, and David who have let me tell them fairy tales, who have learned to love them, and who at their young age don't know anything about anti-fairy tales as yet.

University of Vermont **Wolfgang Mieder**
Burlington, Vermont
Spring 1985

I. SENSE OF FAIRY TALES

CHESTER SIMON KALLMAN

Tellers of Tales

Tales of the folk? Long may their creeds inspire
Uncommon terror, that all may own
What, wrought by one man sitting alone,
May please his neighbors round a common fire.

SARA HENDERSON HAY

The Benefactors

Do not delude yourself that they are kind,
Or think for a single moment they forget
The terms of the agreement—they'll remind
The unfortunate debtor of his reckless debt.
The Miller's conniving Daughter will regret
Her deal with Rumpelstiltskin; and the King
Who promised the Witch to forfeit the first thing
That greeted his safe home-coming will be met

At the gate by his dearest child. Be very sure
Whenever you bargain for your heart's desire,
That whether in sober fact or fairy tale
Grimms' Law of Payment in Full will still prevail.
If not today, then certainly tomorrow,
As many a man discovers, to his sorrow.

SARA HENDERSON HAY

The Princess

I'll ask for a red rose blossoming in the snow,
A music box hid in a walnut shell;
Nine golden apples on a silver bough,
A mirror that can speak, and cast a spell.
I'll send them East of the moon, and West of the sun,
For a wishing ring made of a dragon's claw . . .
And they will fail, just as the rest have done,
And I can stay at home, with dear Papa.

Oh sometimes in my silken bed I wake
All of a shiver, and my hair on end,
Because again the terrible dream occurred:
What if one of those suitors should come back
With the impossible trophy in his hand,
And I should have to keep my foolish word!

LISEL MUELLER

Reading the Brothers Grimm to Jenny

Dead means somebody has to kiss you.

Jenny, your mind commands
kingdoms of black and white:
you shoulder the crow on your left,
the snowbird on your right;
for you the cinders part
and let the lentils through,
and noise falls into place
as screech or sweet roo-coo,
while in my own, real world
gray foxes and gray wolves
bargain eye to eye,
and the amazing dove
takes shelter under the wing
of the raven to keep dry.

Knowing that you must climb,
one day, the ancient tower
where disenchantment binds
the curls of innocence,
that you must live with power
and honor circumstance,
that choice is what comes true—
O, Jenny, pure in heart,
why do I lie to you?

Why do I read you tales
in which birds speak the truth
and pity cures the blind,
and beauty reaches deep
to prove a royal mind?
Death is a small mistake
there, where the kiss revives;
Jenny, we make just dreams
out of our unjust lives.

Still, when your truthful eyes,
your keen, attentive stare,
endow the vacuous slut
with royality, when you match
her soul to her shimmering hair,
what can she do but rise
to your imagined throne?
And what can I, but see
beyond the world that is
when, faithful, you insist
I have the golden key—
and learn from you once more
the terror and the bliss,
the world as it might be?

RANDALL JARRELL

The Märchen

(Grimm's Tales)

Listening, listening; it is never still.
This is the forest: long ago the lives
Edged armed into its tides (the axes were its stone
Lashed with the skins of dwellers to its boughs);
We felled our islands there, at last, with iron.
The sunlight fell to them, according to our wish,
And we believed, till nightfall, in that wish;
And we believed, till nightfall, in our lives.

The bird is silent; but its cold breast stirs
Raggedly, and the gloom the moonlight bars
Is blurred with the fluff its long death strewed
In the crumpled fern; and far off something falls.
If the firs forget their breath, if the leaf that perishes
Holds, a bud, to spring; sleeps, fallen, under snow—
It is never still. The darkness quakes with blood;
From its pulse the dark eyes of the hunter glow
Green as their forest, fading images
Of the dream in the firelight: shudder of the coals
In their short Hell, vined skeleton
Of the charcoal-burner dozing in the snow.
Hänsel, to map the hard way, cast his bones
Up clouds to Paradise; His sparrows ate
And he plunged home, past peat and measures, to his
kin
Furred in the sooty darkness of the cave
Where the old gods nodded. How the devil's beard
Coiled round the dreaming Hänsel, till his limbs
Grew gnarled as a fakir's on the spindling Cross
The missions rowed from Asia: eternal corpse
Of the Scapegoat, gay with His blood's watered beads,
Red wax in the new snow (strange to His warmed stare);
The wooden mother and the choir of saints, His stars;
And God and His barons, always, iron behind.
Gorged Hänsel felt His blood burn thin as air
In a belly swollen with the airy kine;
How many ages boiled Christ's bark for soup!
Giddy with emptiness, a second wife

Scolding the great-eyed children of a ghost,
He sends them, in his tale, not out to death
(Godfather Death, the reaping messenger),
Nor to the devil cringing in the gloom,
Shifting his barred hooves with a crunch like snow—
But to a king: the blind untroubled Might
Renting a destiny to men on terms—
Come, mend me and wed half of me, my son!
Behind, the headsman fondles his gnawn block.
So men have won a kingdom—there are kings;
Are giants, warlocks, the unburied dead
Invulnerable to any power—the Necessity
Men spring from, die under: the unbroken wood.

Noon, the gold sun of hens and aldermen
Inked black as India, on the green ground,
Our patterns, homely, mercenary, magnified—
Bewitching as the water of Friar Bacon's glass.
(*Our* farmer fooled the devil with a turnip,
Our tailor won a queen with seven flies;
Mouser and mousie and a tub of fat
Kept house together—and a louse, a louse
Brewed small beer in an eggshell with a flea.)
But at evening the poor light, far-off, fantastic—
Sun of misers and of mermen, the last foolish gold
Of soldiers wandering through the country with a
crutch—
Scattered its leagues of shadows on the plots
Where life, horned sooty lantern patched with eyes,
Hides more than it illumines, dreams the hordes
Of imps and angels, all of its own hue.
In the great world everything is just the same
Or just the opposite, we found (we never went).
The tinkers, peddlers brought their pinch of salt:
In our mouths the mill of the unresting sea
Ground till their very sores were thirsty.
Quaking below like quicksand, there is fire—
The dowser's twig dips not to water but to Hell;

And the Father, uncomfortable overseer,
Shakes from the rain-clouds Heaven's branding bolt.
Beyond, the Alps ring, avalanche on avalanche,
And the lost palmers freeze to bliss, a smile
Baring their poor teeth, blackened as the skulls
Of sanctuaries—splinters of the Cross, the Ark, the Tree
Jut from a saint's set jawbone, to put out
With one bought vision many a purging fire.
As the circles spread, the stone hopes like a child.
The weak look to the helpless for their aid—
The beasts who, ruled by their god, Death,
Bury the son with their enchanted thanks
For the act outside their possibility:
The victim spared, the labors sweated through, for love
Neither for mate nor litter, but for—anything.
When had it mattered whom we helped? It always paid.
When the dead man's heart broke they found written
there
(He could not write): *The wish has made it so.*
Or so he wished. The platter appliquéd
With meals for parents, scraps for children, gristle
For Towser, a poor dog; the walnut jetting wine;
The broom that, fretting for a master, swept a world;
The spear that, weeping for a master, killed a child;
And gold to bury, from the deepest mines—
These neither to wisdom nor to virtue, but to Grace,
The son remembered in the will of God—
These were wishes. The glass in which I saw
Somewhere else, someone else: the field upon which
sprawled
Dead, and the ruler of the dead, my twin—
Were wishes? Hänsel, by the eternal sea,
Said to the flounder for his first wish, *Let me wish*
And let my wish be granted; it was granted.
Granted, granted. . . . Poor Hänsel, once too powerless
To shelter your own children from the cold
Or quiet their bellies with the thinnest gruel,
It was not power that you lacked, but wishes.

Had you not learned—have we not learned, from tales
Neither of beasts nor kingdoms nor their Lord,
But of our own hearts, the realm of death—
Neither to rule nor die? to change, to change!

ALFRED CORN

Dreambooks

Out of the unreal shadows of the night comes back the real life that we had known. We have to resume it where we had left off and there steals over us a terrible sense of necessity for the continuance of energy in the same wearisome round of stereotyped habits, or a wild longing, it may be, that our eyelids might open some morning upon a world that had been re-fashioned anew in the darkness for our pleasure, a world in which things would have fresh shapes and colours, and be changed, or have other secrets . . .

OSCAR WILDE

A cold night held the clandestine—
After eight o'clock all books were banned.
Under cover, transfixed, I read
And memorized fables by flashlight.
Dream-confections shone in that pale
Epergne of light—tidbit, chestnut,
Nosegay, marzipan *fantaisie*.
Daytime misfits, the balls (flame-stitched),
The bats (oak) that always withered
In my hands, convicted as frauds,
Left me to my bed companions
(None as sticky as the Hardy boys):
Andersen, Grimm, Lewis Carroll.

Perfect programs for tone epics
By Mahler, pure nightmare fodder—
Limbs severed in the Black Forest;
Caesarenwahnsinn of the Red Queen;
The fishwife who tried to be Ms. God;
The Match Girl, burning and freezing;
The six enchanted Swan Brothers . . .
A flock of possible illusions.
Bluffest comforter against cold,
Each story exploded in brief
Artificial fire, then vanished,
Resuming limbo—until next
Reading.
            Now for the sandstar-spill:
Clumsy duckling clasps all his matches
In a fist, loneliness-, hunger-, cold-

Defying, urchin's inkling of death.
Images ignite a blue gas-ring,
Aster-halo, Paradise headgear.

Not Paradise or Limbo. Hades,
A theater of rounds and riddles.
Dreambook, opened to read the future, where
A painful few will have the courage
of their imagination and live
By it. Reared on absurdities,
To whom the usual was ludicrous,
I naturally accept the first
Person of the Dream: *Snow Queen, dragged up*
From the Frozen Lake of Betrayal.
Brittle spectre, scattering eye-splinters
Of diamond, an icon in ermine,
Lace and pearls . . . Those glass eyes know me—
From some old hex party probably.

What should be my hand is extended
As—surprise—an aigrette. But of course,
I'm the sixth son, bird imperfectly
Sleeved in a shirt of nettles: part swan,
With an artless limb, flight-worthy, if laming
And useless for swordplay—or base hits.
In my chest I feel a lump of ice.

Grim fairytale. "Once upons" are always
Puns, double understandings for
The double life, to be read and dreamed
Until the secret order appears.

Night turned the page: dawn would reveal
A figure like a frozen bird
Buried in drifts of wool. Burnt out,

Its battery dead, the flash lay
To one side. A mirror opposing,
All too lucid, reflected gray
Squares of light. Morning announced its
Fictions, a steeplechase laid out
Straight, as on a chessboard, instincts
Reversed in glass. Off with that wing!
Another day's prose to get through.

II. FAIRY TALE POTPOURRIS

HELEN CHASIN

Mythics

I. Ondine

All the cautionary tales of strange girls
could not prevent coming to this:
sea-changed, I dance in shallows
dripping feathery anklets
and splash in the tide (foamy,
opalescent) weedy hair eddying
in its elemental pull,
the fish princess who asked for legs
and bled into her footprints,
her scaly heart flaking until dawn.

II. Cinderella

In this domicile of cosmetic disasters
(dowager's hump, psoriasis, spinster's
breath, dropped arches) I queen it
over the slag heap, over the resident
hags. None of theirs! Changeling
beauty, domestic burden: I sift coal
like black diamonds—alien, determined
to make it out of this dreary household.

III. Rapunzel

Removed by that crone
I range in my cloister, closeted with
dreams of release, growing my hair
like foliage, gathering moss.
Ugly, covetous, my keeper rages at her ward,
her golden girl. Our bramble thickets lock
into a wall and darken my chamber.
You might find me
and I unbraid to your call,
glory in the fall of my crowning glory,
drop into living with my blind, punished hero.

IV. Rumpelstiltskin

I took instruction in love's ravel,
fabricated a homespun treasure
and dazzled my greedy regent into husbandry.
After the baby, complications set in.
Pursued by my useful, anonymous menace
and spinning frantic names, I twisted
in our blood bargain until a minister
told his funny story: how
the little man wove his grotesque forest circle,
the gleeful warp of my answer.
And when, dancing into a tantrum
he dropped out of the riddle
I kept my king, gold, child, and secret.

V. Snow White

Fled from the battle, hid
from the wicked queen's fatal plot,
I lie low and make do
with beauty and virtue
and cohabit with small men: friendly,
inadequate. This house,
my woodsy retreat, is easy
to keep in order. What could be more
innocent, except to dream,
latent and clothed, under glass
until the prince and his retinue
jar my crib and I am roused,
passive, saved?

VI. Psyche

In these nights, transported, I know
love's perfection: words like the heart's choke,
body's language, framed like a dream,
the ultimate dark secret.
Women have risked burning
for hours less extraordinary than these.
Love, waiting for your visit
I long for the dailiness, human rubs, usual
trials and flawed pleasures
this perpetual ecstasy denies.

VII. Beauty (and the Beast)

Whether it was the maxims about good hearts
and the limited value of pure esthetics
or something closer to danger—
once I saw him, the princelings and precepts went
neutral as oatmeal. He was ugly as sin:
animal heavings, flaccid mouth, agonized baboon stare,
pitted skin, hairshirted like a mistaken birth.
My cry mimicked pity.
Ladies, all's fair in
ignorance; I was young and easily moved.
Now, rewarded, I submit to his transfiguration.

JANE FLANDERS

Fairy Tales

Bound by unnatural sleep
Still I hear you hacking at briars
Tasting of blood, you kiss me
On a rumpled bed

You come again shaggy, uncouth
Feathered, covered with slime, you ask
Can I love such beastliness
And I say no

Look for the stairless tower
When you call my name I will let down my hair
And draw you up like a bucket
Of fresh water

GAIL WHITE

Happy Endings

Red Riding Hood and her grandmother
made the wolf
into a big fur coat
and Gretel
shoved Hansel into the oven
and ate him with the witch
and the Beauty enjoyed
her long sleep
quite as much
as the awakening kiss
and the Prince might take
Cinderella to the palace
but she would insist
on scrubbing floors
and scouring pots
and getting her good clothes
covered with ashes
after all
it was what
she was used to.

DANNIE ABSE

Pantomime Diseases

When the fat Prince french-kissed Sleeping Beauty
her eyelids opened wide. She heard applause,
the photographer's shout, wedding guest laughter.
Poor girl—she married the Prince out of duty
and suffered insomnia ever after.

The lies of Once-upon-a-Time appal.
Cinderella seeing white mice grow into horses
shrank to the wall—an event so ominous
she didn't go to the Armed Forces Ball
but phoned up Alcoholics Anonymous.

Snow White suffered from profound anaemia;
the genie warned, 'Aladdin you'll go blind,'
when the little lad gleefully rubbed his lamp;
the Babes in the Wood died of pneumonia;
D. Whittington turned back because of cramp.

And schoolmaster Jack, behind the sheds, caressed
schoolgirl Jill, one third his age and pantless.
Then, panting, they went up the hill and back
till Cupid's leaden arrow in his chest
caused a flutter, a major heart attack.

When the three Darling children thought they'd fly
to Never-Never Land—the usual trip—
their pin-point pupils betrayed addiction;
and not hooked by Captain Hook but by
that ponce, Peter Pan! All the rest is fiction.

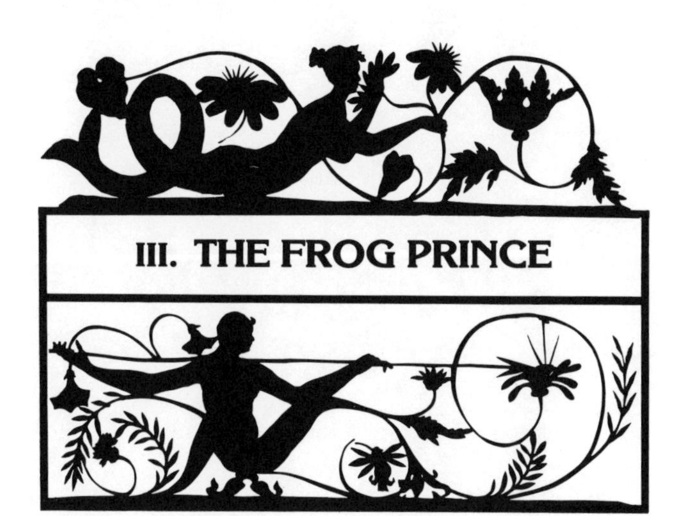

III. THE FROG PRINCE

SARA HENDERSON HAY

The Marriage

The King and I are more than satisfied;
It's turned out better than we ever hoped.
He's good to her, she made a lovely bride.
And think how we'd have felt, if they'd eloped!
We're quite aware of what his motives were:
He wanted money, and an easy life,
But in the end we had to humor her,
And all she wanted was to be his wife.

As for that fairy tale she likes to tell
About the Frog who scrambled from the well
And gave her back her ball, all dripping wet,
Then turned into a Prince (that's how they met),
We know he's not a Prince—the point is this:
Our poor romantic daughter thinks he is.

ROBERT GRAVES

The Frog and the Golden Ball

She let her golden ball fall down the well
And begged a cold frog to retrieve it;
For which she kissed his ugly, gaping mouth—
Indeed, he could scarce believe it.

And seeing him transformed to his princely shape,
Who had been by hags enchanted,
She knew she could never love another man
Nor by any fate be daunted.

But what would her royal father and mother say?
They had promised her in marriage
To a cousin whose wide kingdom marched with theirs,
Who rode in a jewelled carriage.

'Our plight, dear heart, would appear past human hope
To all except you and me: to all
Who have never swum as a frog in a dark well
Or have lost a golden ball.'

'What then shall we do now?' she asked her lover.
He kissed her again, and said:
'Is magic of love less powerful at your Court
Than at this green well-head?'

STEVIE SMITH

The Frog Prince

I am a frog,
I live under a spell,
I live at the bottom
Of a green well.

And here I must wait
Until a maiden places me
On her royal pillow,
And kisses me,
In her father's palace.

The story is familiar,
Everybody knows it well,
But do other enchanted people feel as nervous
As I do? The stories do not tell,

Ask if they will be happier
When the changes come,
As already they are fairly happy
In a frog's doom?

I have been a frog now
For a hundred years
And in all this time
I have not shed many tears,

I am happy, I like the life,
Can swim for many a mile
(When I have hopped to the river)
And am for ever agile.

And the quietness,
Yes, I like to be quiet
I am habituated
To a quiet life,

But always when I think these thoughts,
As I sit in my well
Another thought comes to me and says:
It is part of the spell

To be happy
To work up contentment
To make much of being a frog
To fear disenchantment

Says, It will be *heavenly*
To be set free,
Cries, *Heavenly* the girl who disenchants
And the royal times, *heavenly,*
And I think it will be.

Come, then, royal girl and royal times,
Come quickly,
I can be happy until you come
But I cannot be heavenly,
Only disenchanted people
Can be heavenly.

HYACINTHE HILL

Rebels from Fairy Tales

We are the frogs who will not turn to princes.
We will not change our green and slippery skin
for one so lily-pale and plain, so smooth
it seems to have no grain. We will not leave
our leap, our spring, accordion. We have
seen ourselves in puddles, and we like
our grin. Men are so up and down, so thin
they look like walking trees. Their knees seem stiff,
and we have seen men shooting hares and deer.
They're queer . . . they even war with one another!
They've stretched too far from earth and natural things
for us to admire. We prefer to lie
close to the water looking at the sky
reflected; contemplating how the sun,
Great Rana, can thrust his yellow, webbed foot
through all the elements in a giant jump;
can poke the bottom of the brook; warm
the stumps for us to sit upon; and heat
our backs. Men have forgotten to relax.
They bring their noisy boxes, and the blare
insults the air. We cannot hear the cheer
of crickets, nor our own dear booming chugs.
Frogs wouldn't even eat men's legs.
We scorn their warm, dry princesses. We're proud
of our own bug-eyed brides with bouncing strides.
Keep your magic. We are not such fools.
Here is the ball without a claim on it.
We may begin from the same tadpoles, but
we've thought a bit, and will not turn to men.

PHYLLIS THOMPSON

A Fairy Tale

Prince, when I found you downwind of the toadstools
In the spring wood clearing, gaping with heartache,
And you gulped, swollen under your sad jewels,
I took you in a cold passion, for pity's sake,

For the ludicrous white belly and bulging head.
You jumped, suddenly, long green legs outsplayed,
To my cupped hand. So was I brought to bed
By a pledge, my white flesh by your green skin laid.

How shall I tell the shapely change that fell
On us as we embraced, reluctant? When
You kiss my glistening skin I feel a spell
Dissolve, and I come green to your hands again.

I do not know the seeming from the true
As we slip into our unambiguous climax!
I, last and loveliest born, most happy—you,
Prince, still humped like a frog in the slime of sex!

JOHN N. MILLER

Prince Charming

Let them call me "froggy," "wart-face," or
"Hopalong castoff"—I bear my secret
Meekly enough. Behind my shy croak, somewhere
Deep within this spelled flesh, lies the Real Me.

It bides its time. Society, I know,
Bewitched by suave appearances, can never
Hope to recognize a noble soul.
So, hunching my green-mottled skin, I savor

Dreams of love—my Little Princess who
Someday must clasp me, kiss me, then know
My worth. I feel her lips against the cool
Slime of my mouth, my webbed toes

Twitch at the thought—ah, love! And yet, and yet . . .
Think what a prince lies hidden. What if she's
The wrong one? what if I commit
Myself, my noble essence, to her pleased

But childish eyes? No, no. Let my comrades still
View me as "frog-face" here in these scummed
Environs, if thereby they will
Shield me; let no slack lips dispel my charm.

ANNE SEXTON

The Frog Prince

Frau Doktor,
Mama Brundig,
take out your contacts,
remove your wig.

I write for you.
I entertain.
But frogs come out
of the sky like rain.

Frogs arrive
With an ugly fury.
You are my judge.
You are my jury.

My guilts are what
we catalogue.
I'll take a knife
and chop up frog.

Frog has no nerves.
Frog is as old as a cockroach.
Frog is my father's genitals.
Frog is a malformed doorknob.
Frog is a soft bag of green.

The moon will not have him.
The sun wants to shut off
like a light bulb.
At the sight of him
the stone washes itself in a tub.
The crow thinks he's an apple
and drops a worm in.
At the feel of frog
the touch-me-nots explode
like electric slugs.

Slime will have him.
Slime has made him a house.

Mr. Poison
is at my bed.
He wants my sausage.
He wants my bread.

Mama Brundig,
he wants my beer.
He wants my Christ
for a souvenir.

Frog has boil disease
and a bellyful of parasites.
   He says: Kiss me. Kiss me.
   And the ground soils itself.

Why
should a certain
quite adorable princess
be walking in her garden
at such a time
and toss her golden ball
up like a bubble
and drop it into the well?
It was ordained.
Just as the fates deal out
the plague with a tarot card.
Just as the Supreme Being drills
holes in our skulls to let
the Boston Symphony through.

But I digress.
A loss has taken place.
The ball has sunk like a cast-iron pot
into the bottom of the well.

Lost, she said,
my moon, my butter calf,
my yellow moth, my Hindu hare.
Obviously it was more than a ball.
Balls such as these are not
for sale in Au Bon Marché.
I took the moon, she said,
between my teeth
and now it is gone
and I am lost forever.
A thief had robbed by day.

Suddenly the well grew
thick and boiling
and a frog appeared.
His eyes bulged like two peas
and his body was trussed into place.
Do not be afraid, Princess,
he said, I am not a vagabond,
a cattle farmer, a shepherd,
a doorkeeper, a postman
or a laborer.
I come to you as a tradesman.
I have something to sell.
Your ball, he said,
for just three things.
Let me eat from your plate.
Let me drink from your cup.
Let me sleep in your bed.
She thought, Old Waddler,
those three you will never do,
but she made the promises
with hopes for her ball once more.
He brought it up in his mouth
like a tricky old dog
and she ran back to the castle
leaving the frog quite alone.

That evening at dinner time
a knock was heard at the castle door
and a voice demanded:
King's youngest daughter,
let me in. You promised;
now open to me.
I have left the skunk cabbage
and the eels to live with you:
The king then heard of her promise
and forced her to comply.
The frog first sat on her lap.
He was as awful as an undertaker.
Next he was at her plate
looking over her bacon
and calves' liver.

We will eat in tandem,
he said gleefully.
Her fork trembled
as if a small machine
had entered her.
He sat upon the liver
and partook like a gourmet.
The princess choked
as if she were eating a puppy.
From her cup he drank.
It wasn't exactly hygienic.
From her cup she drank
as if it were Socrates' hemlock.

Next came the bed.
The silky royal bed.
Ah! The penultimate hour!
There was the pillow
with the princess breathing
and there was the sinuous frog
riding up and down beside her.
I have been lost in a river
of shut doors, he said,

and I have made my way over
the wet stones to live with you.
She woke up aghast.
I suffer for birds and fireflies
but not frogs, she said,
and threw him across the room.
Kaboom!

Like a genie coming out of a samovar,
a handsome prince arose in the
corner of her royal bedroom.
He had kind eyes and hands
and was a friend of sorrow.
Thus they were married.
After all he had compromised her.

He hired a night watchman
so that no one could enter the chamber
and he had the well
boarded over so that
never again would she lose her ball,
that moon, that Krishna hair,
that blind poppy, that innocent globe,
that madonna womb.

PHOEBE PETTINGELL

Frog Prince

They say you were made in your father's image:
But I know better,
Having seen you born
Croaking and splaying into that brighter light than
  morning;
I sensed, then, you were not human,
But some primal creature
Come from my sloughy darkness—a succubus
  nourished on
My own badness, and I,
The witch-mother, who made
This bleak transformation of passion into such repulsive
  matter.

Great tadpole head and mouth! with a walleyed reptilian
  glare,
You ogled me in cold-blooded dislike,
Informing me of my mistake
In having ever dredged you out of your sunless pond;
Yet did not hesitate to take
From me all that I had to give,
That you might live, gorged and bloated, on my
  grudging love;
And now, sucked dry, I am abandoned
By my monarch-monster, left vainly to wish
That I could be the princess whose kiss will change you
  into a man.

ELIZABETH BREWSTER

The Princess Addresses the Frog Prince

Oh, Frog Prince, Frog Prince,
it was not for you
that I dropped my golden ball
down into the deep water.

It was only by chance
that I dropped it at all.
I intended to stand still
holding the ball safe in my hand
and to look at myself reflected
with my gold crown on my hair
in the pond's surface.

Never in all the stories
was there a more beautiful princess.

And when the ball slipped
and fell from my hand
among the water lilies,
if I expected anyone to rise
from beneath the water

it was a merman or a drowned prince
who would be brought to life
by my eyes.

Never mind, you have a fine voice.
I will take you out of the water
to play in my garden.
I will even take you into the palace.
You shall sit by my gold plate
at dinner time
and be my ugly pet
and sing me songs.

PAUL R. JONES

Becoming a Frog

no one is home today doing usual chores.
my body sweats mucus onto the skin.
they are all at the seashore going for a swim.

i strut away my legs becoming stiff.
did he lift that curtain to check me out?
a sound bubbles to my lips but held back.

she knows him well enough to ask for a dance.
webs form between all of the extremities.
they grow a garden for vegetables.

lower my hand comes away from the floor sucking.
she would be making dinner for herself now.
my throat swells so air collects in it.

she asked me if i knew her from some time ago.
i said she looked familiar.
she went wondering if i was high-born.

small stone-dropped ripples are tidal.
they heard me leave with an obvious noise.
i will go up there and continuously breathe.

SUSAN MITCHELL

From the Journals of the Frog Prince

In March I dreamed of mud,
sheets of mud over the ballroom chairs and table,
rainbow slicks of mud under the throne.
In April I saw mud of clouds and mud of sun.
Now in May I find excuses to linger in the kitchen
for wafts of silt and ale,
cinnamon and river bottom,
tender scallion and sour underlog.

At night I cannot sleep.
I am listening for the dribble of mud
climbing the stairs to our bedroom
as if a child in a wet bathing suit ran
up them in the dark.

Last night I said, "Face it, you're bored
How many times can you live over
with the same excitement
that moment when the princess leans
into the well, her face a petal
falling to the surface of the water
as you rise like a bubble to her lips,
the golden ball bursting from your mouth?"
Remember how she hurled you against the wall,
your body cracking open,
skin shrivelling to the bone,
the green pod of your heart splitting in two,
and her face imprinted with every moment of your
   transformation?

I no longer tremble.

Night after night I lie beside her.
"Why is your forehead so cool and damp?" she asks.
Her breasts are soft and dry as flour.
The hand that brushes my head is feverish.
At her touch I long for wet leaves,
the slap of water against rocks.

"What were you thinking of?" she asks.
How can I tell her
I am thinking of the green skin
shoved like wet pants behind the Directoire desk?
Or tell her I am mortgaged to the hilt
of my sword, to the leek-green tip of my soul?
Someday I will drag her by her hair
to the river—and what? Drown her?
Show her the green flame of my self rising at her feet?
But there's no more violence in her
than in a fence or a gate.

"What are you thinking of?" she whispers.
I am staring into the garden.
I am watching the moon
wind its trail of golden slime around the oak,
over the stone basin of the fountain.
How can I tell her
I am thinking that transformations are not forever?

ROBERT PACK

The Frog Prince

(A Speculation on Grimm's Fairy Tale)

Imagine the princess' surprise!
Who would have thought a frog's cold frame
Could hold the sweet and gentle body
Of a prince? How can I name
The joy she must have felt to learn
His transformation was the wonder
Of her touch—that she too, in
Her way, had been transformed under
Those clean sheets? Such powers were
Like nothing she had ever read.
And in the morning when her mother
Came and saw them there in bed,
Heard how a frog became a prince;
What was it that her mother said?

GALWAY KINNELL

Kissing the Toad

Somewhere this dusk
a girl puckers her mouth
and considers kissing
the toad a boy has plucked
from the cornfield and hands
her with both hands;
rough and lichenous
but for the immense ivory belly,
like those old entrepreneurs
sprawling on Mediterranean beaches,
with popped eyes,
it watches the girl who might kiss it,
pisses, quakes, tries
to make its smile wider:
to love on, oh yes, to love on.

IV. RAPUNZEL

LOUIS UNTERMEYER

Rapunzel

Let down your hair,
That cloudy-gold lure,
The delicate snare
That holds me secure.
Delight and despair
War with me now—
Let down your hair.

Shake out each curl
Swiftly, and be
Like Spring, a wild girl
With her hair flying free.
Bury me there,
And be buried with me . . .
Let down your hair!

JOY DAVIDMAN

The Princess in the Ivory Tower

The Prince's voice, faint at the edge of sunlight,
where the clear sun leans backward from the night,
thin as a bird, faint as the fading air:

Rapunzel, Rapunzel,
let down your golden hair,

and I will climb up to the height of heaven,
and I will let the wind blow over my shoulder,
and I will let the stars drift through my hands,
coming to the magic house, the ivory chamber,
coming into the circle of dreams and drowning mist,
and wind will blow out both the witch's eyes.

Rapunzel,
let down your golden hair,

make a ladder for me to enter heaven,
make a ladder for me to dally with the stars,
make a stairway through the dizzy air.
There shall be no root upon the earth for my stair
and I shall sway between the sun and moon
and all the merry stars shall ring in tune
when I come in, when I come to the ivory room.

Let down your hair, let down your golden hair,
that I may be free from the murder at my foot,
that I may be free from the truth upon my eyes,
that I may be free from the worm at my heart's root.

SARA HENDERSON HAY

Rapunzel

Oh God, let me forget the things he said.
Let me not lie another night awake
Repeating all the promises he made,
Freezing and burning for his faithless sake;
Seeing his face, feeling his hand once more
Loosen my braided hair until it fell
Shining and free; remembering how he swore
A single strand might lift a man from Hell. . . .

I knew that other girls, in Aprils past,
Had leaned, like me, from some old tower's room
And watched him clamber up, hand over fist. . . .
I knew that I was not the first to twist
Her heartstrings to a rope for him to climb.
I might have known I would not be the last.

ELI MANDEL

Rapunzel

(Girl in a Tower)

Another one of those puzzles
there's not a farmer
skinny as a gold seed
tough as a nutcracker
can plough or crack.

How do towers grow like that?
Overnight: the garden
a green sky, its moon
like beet, its sun
a turnip underground?

Many girls lock themselves up,
become pantries, closets.
Some, like trees, grow bark,
and others, like rivers,
burble into dimpled pools.

But they are not these crooked
wicked towers, not rooms
inside of rooms, not brooms
to thrash out of a seedy man
his golden crop and garden.

I lean on a ladder of hair,
remember the right rhymes,
look up at the green head,
climb toward the turnip-colour sun.

GERARD PREVIN MEYER

Rapunzel Song

Upon the slow descending air
the trees let down their darkened hair;
the leaves are falling, so the night
turning away from what's more bright
may come as a lover to the shade,
wearing the wind.

So once the maid
Rapunzel of the legends found
she'd lifted a lover from the ground
who by her hair, that yellow flame,
ascended.

Who now knows his name?
And was he dark or was he fair?
Only, upon the lovely stair
he met Rapunzel.

Of the night
what more is known, than: on the slight
and windy tresses of the trees
a dark gallant was seen to seize,
amorously began to climb
and mounted swiftly into time.

ANNE SEXTON

Rapunzel

A woman
who loves a woman
is forever young.
The mentor
and the student
feed off each other.
Many a girl
had an old aunt
who locked her in the study
to keep the boys away.
They would play rummy
or lie on the couch
and touch and touch.
Old breast against young breast . . .

Let your dress fall down your shoulder,
come touch a copy of you
for I am at the mercy of rain,
for I have left the three Christs of Ypsilanti,
for I have left the long naps of Ann Arbor
and the church spires have turned to stumps.
The sea bangs into my cloister
for the young politicians are dying,
are dying to hold me, my young dear,
hold me . . .
The yellow rose will turn to cinder
and New York City will fall in
before we are done so hold me,
my young dear, hold me.
Put your pale arms around my neck.
Let me hold your heart like a flower
lest it bloom and collapse.
Give me your skin
as sheer as a cobweb,
let me open it up
and listen in and scoop out the dark.
Give me your nether lips
all puffy with their art

and I will give you angel fire in return.
We are two clouds
glistening in the bottle glass.
We are two birds
washing in the same mirror.
We were fair game
but we have kept out of the cesspool.
We are strong.
We are the good ones.
Do not discover us
for we lie together all in green
like pond weeds.
Hold me, my young dear, hold me.

They touch their delicate watches
one at a time.
They dance to the lute
two at a time.
They are as tender as bog moss.
They play mother-me-do
all day.
A woman
who loves a woman
is forever young.

Once there was a witch's garden
more beautiful than Eve's
with carrots growing like little fish,
with many tomatoes rich as frogs,
onions as ingrown as hearts,
the squash singing like a dolphin
and one patch given over wholly to magic—
rampion, a kind of salad root,
a kind of harebell more potent than penicillin,
growing leaf by leaf, skin by skin,
as rapt and as fluid as Isadora Duncan.
However the witch's garden was kept locked
and each day a woman who was with child

looked upon the rampion wildly,
fancying that she would die
if she could not have it.
Her husband feared for her welfare
and thus climbed into the garden
to fetch the life-giving tubers.

Ah ha, cried the witch,
whose proper name was Mother Gothel,
you are a thief and now you will die.
However they made a trade,
typical enough in those times.
He promised his child to Mother Gothel
so of course when it was born
she took the child away with her.
She gave the child the name Rapunzel,
another name for the life-giving rampion.
Because Rapunzel was a beautiful girl
Mother Gothel treasured her beyond all things.
As she grew older Mother Gothel thought:
None but I will ever see her or touch her.
She locked her in a tower without a door
or a staircase. It had only a high window.
When the witch wanted to enter she cried:
Rapunzel, Rapunzel, let down your hair.
Rapunzel's hair fell to the ground like a rainbow.
It was as yellow as a dandelion
and as strong as a dog leash.
Hand over hand she shinnied up
the hair like a sailor
and there in the stone-cold room,
as cold as a museum,
Mother Gothel cried:
Hold me, my young dear, hold me,
and thus they played mother-me-do.

Years later a prince came by
and heard Rapunzel singing in her loneliness.
That song pierced his heart like a valentine
but he could find no way to get to her.
Like a chameleon he hid himself among the trees
and watched the witch ascend the swinging hair.
The next day he himself called out:
Rapunzel, Rapunzel, let down your hair,
and thus they met and he declared his love.
What is this beast, she thought,
with muscles on his arms
like a bag of snakes?
What is this moss on his legs?
What prickly plant grows on his cheeks?
What is this voice as deep as a dog?
Yet he dazzled her with his answers.
Yet he dazzled her with his dancing stick.
They lay together upon the yellowy threads,
swimming through them
like minnows through kelp
and they sang out benedictions like the Pope.

Each day he brought her a skein of silk
to fashion a ladder so they could both escape.
But Mother Gothel discovered the plot
and cut off Rapunzel's hair to her ears
and took her into the forest to repent.
When the prince came the witch fastened
the hair to a hook and let it down.
When he saw that Rapunzel had been banished
he flung himself out of the tower, a side of beef.
He was blinded by thorns that pricked him like tacks.
As blind as Oedipus he wandered for years
until he heard a song that pierced his heart
like that long-ago valentine.
As he kissed Rapunzel her tears fell on his eyes
and in the manner of such cure-alls
his sight was suddenly restored.

They lived happily as you might expect
proving that mother-me-do
can be outgrown,
just as the fish on Friday,
just as a tricycle.
The world, some say,
is made up of couples.
A rose must have a stem.

As for Mother Gothel,
her heart shrank to the size of a pin,
never again to say: Hold me, my young dear,
hold me,
and only as she dreamt of the yellow hair
did moonlight sift into her mouth.

OLGA BROUMAS

Rapunzel

> *A woman*
> *who loves a woman*
> *is forever young.*
>
> ANNE SEXTON

Climb
through my hair, climb in
to me, love

hovers here like a mother's wish.
You might have been, though you're not
my mother. You let loose like hair, like static
her stilled wish, relentless
in me and constant as
tropical growth. Every hair

on my skin curled up, my spine
an enraptured circuit, a loop of memory, your first
private touch. How many women
have yearned
for our lush perennial, found

themselves pregnant, and had
to subdue their heat, drown out their appetite
with pickles and harsh weeds. How many
grew to confuse greed
with hunger, learned to grow thin on the bitter
root, the mandrake, on their sills, *Old*

bitch, young
darling. May those who speak them
choke on their words, their hunger freeze
in their veins like lard.
Less innocent
in my public youth
than you, less forebearing, I'll break the hush
of our cloistered garden, our harvest continuous

as a moan, the tilled bed luminous
with the future
yield. Red

vows like tulips. Rows
upon rows of kisses from all lips.

V. HANSEL AND GRETEL

NORREYS JEPHSON O'CONOR

To a Child

(With a Copy of the Author's "Hansel and Gretel")

Here, Nancy, let me take your hand,
And lead you back to Fairyland,
In this famed tale of long ago,
Told often in the sunset glow
By mothers, lest their children roam
In the dark forest, far from home.
This lesson learn: that mothers know
Where lurks, perchance, a hidden foe;
And though you may not understand
The reason in each kind command,
It is to keep you from the fear
That terrified the children here.
Learn, too, how God's own angels keep
Your ways by day, your dreams, asleep.

DOROTHY LEE RICHARDSON

Modern Grimm

"Nibble, nibble, little mouse,
Who is nibbling at my house?"
"Only the wind.
Only the wind."

"What have you sown, O darling children?
What have you grown in the land of magic?"
"Only the wind. Only the wind."

"What chroma of wind, O clever children?
What brilliant shade have you made with your magic?
What color of wind?"

"A rich red wind over Hiroshima,
Darkly blowing, brightly glowing.
A red-black wind

"We have sown the wind. Its seed we found
And dropped it lightly to the ground.
We have sown the wind.

"The small thing split. It branched to bear
A thousand red-black fruits in air.
We have sown the wind.

"We have sown the wind. It rises high
Till it beats the ear and blinds the eye
And sweeps a hole in the crouching sky
Where the whirlwind rushes in!"

"Nibble, nibble, little mouse,
Who is nibbling at my house?"
"Only the wind.
Only the wind."

WILLIAM DICKEY

The Dolls Play at Hansel and Gretel

I

They hunch their heads against the fable of night,
Their thin wax heads with eyes that are too large;
Each one examines the bruises of the day.

When they are through with this they take their parts;
This one is witch and this one is the wood,
Trees flit into his huddled brain, and owls.

And the poor children, the senseless, shabby things,
Cluttered with pebbles that will do no good,
Lift their rag hands and imitate despair:

"Why have you put us out into the cold:
All day, helpless as any human child,
We have been yours to fondle or destroy.

You made us saints or thieves or prostitutes,
You put us slyly in Jocasta's bed;
Mother and father, what we are is yours.

We fought the wars you could not fight alone,
But at the end of the garden you said go,
And we sprawled nameless in the pitying flowers.

Now in the dark the *Doppelgänger* winks
To say the path goes on as it always has.
Bushes take foot, and the wood closes in."

II. The Witch's Song

In the epileptic fit
When your bones were scarcely knit
You beheld the paradise
Of my parti-colored eyes.

In the foul delirium
When the cockatrices come,
Eager to delay the truth
You have kissed my withered mouth.

Now let hand release its hold
On the world you have been told,
Let the sleeping eyelid fall
Shutting out the sight of all.

Coiling in the middle ear,
Let my word be what you hear,
Let my hand that sews and clips
Snip your tongue and stitch your lips.

In my body you will find
Mathematics of the blind,
Malformations there and scars
Of the potent integers.

In the crevice of my gown
Secret lies your mortal town,
In the science of my breast
Is your formula of rest.

III. The Gingerbread House's Song

Wind the thread and wind the thread,
Mother married with a sailor,
And I thought that I was dead
If her common sense could fail her.
But I buttoned up my fright
And I strangled him at night.

Turn the spool and turn the spool,
Father took a witch for daughter.
Then I knew he was a fool—
Witches can't cross running water.
Like an angel in a dream
I immersed her in the stream.

Sing the song and sing the song,
All the nightingales are hidden.
Right is right and wrong is wrong,
Folk must do what they are bidden
Or I take them by the neck
And I put them in my sack.

Cast the stone and cast the stone,
Eat the muscle and the marrow,
Eat the body to the bone,
It will rise again tomorrow
Worshiping the hand that slew,
And had every right to do.

Close the eye and close the eye,
All things come to him that wishes.
Now the world is only I
I am finding it delicious.
Powerful, virile, handsome, young,
I taste the blood upon my tongue.

IV. The Oven's Song

The toad
Glitters in the night
From the jewel in its head.
Everything else is dead.
I did not bring you.
I will not take you.
Fancies of lunacy glitter in your head.

Only the same door
From the same room and into the same room.
Under this time
It is the same time that it was before
When you came and will come.
Circle the stone with marks to mark your time.
You will remember nothing of them here.

Only the box,
And the locks,
And the nail.
You are unwounded yet, but you will fail.
As soon as you start to know, the wounds will come,
Blood in the pricked thumb,
Blood on the shirt,
Till all of you is drained and put aside,
Folded like paper on a shelf.

You are yourself.
Cuddle into my entrail and be still.
There is no tie between you and my will,
But an indifference.
What you hear
Runs on as steady in my ear
As the noise made by an indifferent machine.
I will not say what you have been,
That is concern, and I am not concerned.
I am the toad's jewel in the center of the skull.
I am what you have earned.

V

Their thin wax heads are scattered on the grass,
Their button eyes look dully at the sky
Where it has begun to rain. The morning comes.

Empty and destitute, they disarrange
The order of life, until the children come
Telling them what are their identities.

SARA HENDERSON HAY

Juvenile Court

Deep in the oven, where the two had shoved her,
They found the Witch, burned to a crisp, of course.
And when the police had decently removed her,
They questioned the children, who showed no remorse.
"She threatened us," said Hansel, "with a kettle
Of boiling water, just because I threw
The cat into the well." Cried little Gretel,
"She fussed because I broke her broom in two,

And said she'd lock up Hansel in a cage
For drawing funny pictures on her fence . . ."
Wherefore the court, considering their age,
And ruling that there seemed some evidence
The pair had acted under provocation,
Released them to their parents, on probation.

DAVID RAY

Hansel and Gretel Return

Now it is time to be cut out
Of the wolf's belly.

It is time to come back home
With what one has brought

For those who were neither charming
Nor caring.

It is time to tell all the tales
To a better night

And to thank especially the extra-
Human, the birds along the way,

The dove that led through the forest,
The duck that let first your sister

And then you ride across the
Dangerous river. It is time

For reunions that are themselves
Compromises. In the firelight

You see the jewels you brought gleam
On the dead as they go on talking.

LOUISE GLÜCK

Gretel in Darkness

This is the world we wanted.
All who would have seen us dead
are dead. I hear the witch's cry
break in the moonlight through a sheet
of sugar: God rewards.
Her tongue shrivels into gas. . . .

Now, far from women's arms
and memory of women, in our father's hut
we sleep, are never hungry.
Why do I not forget?
My father bars the door, bars harm
from this house, and it is years.

No one remembers. Even you, my brother,
summer afternoons you look at me as though
you meant to leave,
as though it never happened.
But I killed for you. I see armed firs,
the spires of that gleaming kiln—

Nights I turn to you to hold me
but you are not there.
Am I alone? Spies
hiss in the stillness, Hansel,
we are there still and it is real, real,
that black forest and the fire in earnest.

ROBIN MORGAN

The Two Gretels

The two Gretels were exploring the forest.
Hansel was home,
sending up flares.

Sometimes one Gretel got afraid.
She said to the other Gretel,
"I think I'm afraid."
"Of course we are," Gretel replied.

Sometimes the other Gretel whispered,
with a shiver,
"You think we should turn back?"
To which her sister Gretel answered,
"We can't. We forgot the breadcrumbs."

So, they went forward
because
they simply couldn't imagine the way back.

And eventually, they found the Gingerbread House,
and the Witch, who was really, they discovered,
the Great Good Mother Goddess,
and they all lived happily ever after.

The Moral of this story is:

Those who would have the whole loaf,
let alone the House,
had better throw away their breadcrumbs.

JOHN OWER

The Gingerbread House

We made our little girl
A gingerbread house.
Despite sweet cement
It leaned as if it yielded
To a hurricane wind.
Our baby took one look at it,
Said it was a witch's house,
And burst into tears.
She was a prophet in her way.
During our estrangement
The witch flew out the window
Riding on the storm.
She cast a wicked spell
That made us hate each other.
And now between the two of us
In the finest fashion
Of the old fairy-tales
We gobble up our child.

VI. CINDERELLA

DOROTHY E. REID

Coach into Pumpkin

They never knew or never cared to know
Why Ellen stirred the coals so wistfully
In early evening, when the flame was low;
They never saw, and would have laughed to see
The tattered book she read and read again
For breathless words of slippers and a prince.
When she grew older, she would look at men
With quick surmising interest; but since
Young Elmer wed and took her to his farm
Ellen has grown more meek, and settled down
To honest labour. There was not much harm
In her quaint notions, for she cut the gown
That she was married in, all frills and laces,
Up into christening dresses for her brood.
At first she used to sit in quiet places
And moon alone, between the beds and food;
But now she rocks quiescent, mending holes,
And never seems to see between her lashes
Young Eleanora lingering by the coals
To poke a wistful finger in the ashes.

ELIZABETH MADOX ROBERTS

Cinderella's Song

Oh, little cat beside my stool,
My tabby cat, my ashy one,
I'll tell you something in your ear,
It's I can put the slipper on.

The cinders all will brush away,
Oh, little cat beside my chair,
And I am very beautiful
When I comb down my hair.

My dress was gold, my dress was blue,
But you can hardly think of that.
My dress came to me through the air,
Oh, little cinder cat.

My dress is gone a little while,
My dress was sweet and blue and cool,
But it will come again to me,
Oh, little cat beside my stool.

ELEANOR FARJEON

Coach

There was a yellow pumpkin
Born on a pumpkin-patch,
As clumsy as a 'potamus,
As coarse as a cottage-thatch.
It longed to be a gooseberry,
A greengage, or a grape,
It longed to give another scent
And have another shape.
The roses looked askance at it,
The lilies looked away—
"This thing is neither fruit nor flower!"
Their glances seemed to say.

One shiny night of midsummer,
When even fairies poach,
A good one waved her wand and said,
"O Pumpkin! be a coach!"
A coach of gold! a coach of glass!
A coach with satin lined!
If you should seek a thousand years,
Such you would not find.
The Princess in her crystal shoes
Eager for the dance
Stepped inside the pumpkin-coach
And rolled to her romance.

The roses reached out after it,
The lilies looked its way—
"O that we were pumpkins too!"
Their glances seemed to say.

EDITH WEAVER

Lost Cinderella

Little rich girl, glittering with bells,
come running lightly as
the fawn of the fairytales
treading musical leaves;

come running through the precious path
in the hypnotic forest
where nothing dares fall into a clutter of death
till you are past,

where the wind stands straight as an elm
to offer fringed shelter
and pale blossoms smile through an atmosphere
glossy as water.

The wolves and the witches will not deign
to lift their muzzles
from counting a spoil of screaming bone
to taste a tinkerbell

and your fortunate body has no skeleton
but cakes and perfume
that wrinkles the noses of neighboring children
who do not know you

But primly wait in the summerhouse
for the promised party
side by side with a council of solemn dolls
who try you in memory.

Why do you who seem freedom herself
crouch in a corner
of the nightmare, the guilty fireplace
in your father's manor:

why have you bartered your flickering dance for sorrow,
to willfully huddle
sobbing over the fallen sparrow
in your belled hand's cradle?

RANDALL JARRELL

Cinderella

Her imaginary playmate was a grown-up
In sea-coal satin. The flame-blue glances,
The wings gauzy as the membrane that the ashes
Draw over an old ember—as the mother
In a jug of cider—were a comfort to her.
They sat by the fire and told each other stories.

"What men want. . . ." said the godmother softly—
How she went on it is hard for a man to say.
Their eyes, on their Father, were monumental marble.
Then they smiled like two old women, bussed each
   other,
Said, "Gossip, gossip"; and, lapped in each other's
   looks,
Mirror for mirror, drank a cup of tea.

Of cambric tea. But there is a reality
Under the good silk of the good sisters'
Good ball gowns. *She* knew. . . . Hard-breasted, naked-
   eyed,
She pushed her silk feet into glass, and rose within
A gown of imaginary gauze. The shy prince drank
A toast to her in champagne from her slipper.

And breathed, "Bewitching!" Breathed, "I am
   bewitched!"
—She said to her godmother, "Men!"
And, later, looking down to see her flesh
Look back up from under lace, the ashy gauze
And pulsing marble of a bridal veil,
She wished it all a widow's coal-black weeds.

A sullen wife and a reluctant mother,
She sat all day in silence by the fire.
Better, later, to stare past her sons' sons,
Her daughters' daughters, and tell stories to the fire.
But best, dead, damned, to rock forever
Beside Hell's fireside—to see within the flames

The Heaven to whose gold-gauzed door there comes
A little dark old woman, the God's Mother,
And cries, "Come in, come in! My son's out now,
Out now, will be back soon, may be back never,
Who knows, eh? *We* know what they are—men, men!
But come, come in till then! Come in till then!

CYNTHIA PICKARD

Cinderella

It was too dark in the chimney corner to see
Whether the floors I scrubbed ever had any shine;
When the food she made me fix turned out not fine
The witch wore out her broom beating me.

She purred for the mirror and gurgled at her beauty
And that of her daughters, but never never mine.
Once I gazed in a bucket of water and thought in
It I saw sparkles. She watched and went Tee Hee.

Then the wonder was. A godmother to the scene!
She was the one, she was the really dear
Who carried a wand whenever she came near
And said: Rest. Be beautiful. Be a queen.
She led me out on a footlog and said *Look*
And lo! a shining brightness was the brook.

SYLVIA PLATH

Cinderella

The prince leans to the girl in scarlet heels,
Her green eyes slant, hair flaring in a fan
Of silver as the rondo slows; now reels
Begin on tilted violins to span

The whole revolving tall glass palace hall
Where guests slide gliding into light like wine;
Rose candles flicker on the lilac wall
Reflecting in a million flagons' shine,

And gilded couples all in whirling trance
Follow holiday revel begun long since,
Until near twelve the strange girl all at once
Guilt-stricken halts, pales, clings to the prince

As amid the hectic music and cocktail talk
She hears the caustic ticking of the clock.

SARA HENDERSON HAY

Interview

Yes, this is where she lived before she won
The title Miss Glass Slipper of the Year,
And went to the ball and married the king's son.
You're from the local press, and want to hear
About her early life? Young man, sit down.
These are my *own* two daughters; you'll not find
Nicer, more biddable girls in all the town,
And lucky, I tell them, not to be the kind

That Cinderella was, spreading those lies,
Telling those shameless tales about the way
We treated her. Oh, nobody denies
That she was pretty, if you like those curls.
But looks aren't everything, I always say.
Be sweet and natural, I tell my girls,
And Mr. Right will come along, some day.

FEROZ AHMED-UD-DIN

Cinderella

This vegetable body drops
down. Vision's lost images
build a palace somewhere,
its marble walls beckoning
barefooted Cinderellas.

When time slips out, smoke
fills lungs and cigarette ends
writhe on the floor. Silently
the doors close behind.

Memory's tinsel silver
glitters in the night.

Here when contracts end
no final handshakes
no grinned goodbyes.
Only moving carriages
that turn into pulp
and mice running through the night.

ANNE HUSSEY

Cinderella Liberated

I sleep with
my feet in the fire
destroying the evidence
one glass shoe
melting like butter
both feet black as briquettes
while the prince
in a world of questions
searches for an answer
he carries near his jewelled sword
the other shoe of the pair
he drinks from it champagne
or Schlitz and that's not
all he does he has
a special pillow for it on his
bed where he polishes it
and in it sees his own
reflection
it has become his talisman his illusion
his astigmatism and his lotus
let no man touch it it's
all he has left
that and this note
dear sir whenever you see
rising from the ashes a bird its feet
blazing like torches
observe closely
it passes for me

MARY BLAKE FRENCH

Ella of the Cinders

I am not physically perfect:
I have no spherical symmetry.
I need no Prince Charming to awaken me.
I am fully conscious of your happily-ever-after!
My feet grow large to break your glass slippers;
I shall use the shivered glass for my own collage.

OLGA BROUMAS

Cinderella

. . . the joy that isn't shared
I heard, dies young.
ANNE SEXTON, 1928–1974

Apart from my sisters, estranged
from my mother, I am a woman alone
in a house of men
who secretly
call themselves princes, alone
with me usually, under cover of dark. I am the one
allowed in

to the royal chambers, whose small foot conveniently
fills the slipper of glass. The woman writer, the lady
umpire, the madam chairman, anyone's wife.
I know what I know.
And I once was glad

of the chance to use it, even alone
in a strange castle, doing overtime on my own, cracking
the royal code. The princes spoke
in their fathers' language, were eager to praise me
my nimble tongue. I am a woman in a state of siege,
alone

as one piece of laundry, strung on a windy clothesline a
mile long. A woman co-opted by promises: the lure
of a job, the ruse of a choice, a woman forced
to bear witness, falsely
against my kind, as each
other sister was judged inadequate, bitchy, incompetent,
jealous, too thin, too fat. I know what I know.
What sweet bread I make

for myself in this prosperous house
is dirty, what good soup I boil turns
in my mouth to mud. Give
me my ashes. A cold stove, a cinder-block pillow, wet
canvas shoes in my sisters', my sisters' hut. Or I swear

I'll die young
like those favored before me, hand-picked each one
for her joyful heart.

ROGER MITCHELL

Cinderella

I

When they found her prostrate in the garden,
talking to a beetle, they locked her in the loft.

There it was spiders. For them, she danced
and made strange noises in her throat.

Nothing could shame her. Tied to the hog trough,
she wallowed in mud and warm moonlight.

At dawn, a sow lay sleeping against her.
She hugged a tree, and they took her clothes away.

She tried to nurse a calf, so they killed it.
And then wiped their hands on her naked breasts.

She would leave all this someday. But for now
she kept to the barn, mooing in the stillness.

II

When she left, she put a tear in a sack
and left it by the back door. It was dawn.

The frog in her palm collected itself
and leapt over the gate.

She would leap like that if she had to.
She would be the fox if the dogs came near.

She followed the ant and the low shrub,
and carried a knife now to bite with.

III

The sisters, naturally, were beautiful.
And, naturally, they were described otherwise.

She knocked on the back door, twice, begging for food.
They stared at her caked thighs, her ropey hair.

One of them threw her a shoe, the other
a cinder, and then watched as she choked them down.

They smiled their smiles in the right places,
but behind the barn they took cats apart.

The boys in the village, though, hung out their tongues
and dreamt. And some of them wept, and some cursed.

She was a broom dressed as a shawl, crouching.
Into her life crept nothing, breathing.

IV

He was not a prince. He was not even rich.
He was a woodcutter, and he drank.

There was no ball, there was no slipper,
and the clock had not yet been invented.

Someone else would think of these things:
the princes and the glass-like elegance,

the indoor bliss and the irreversible
severance from everything living,

the impossible, degrading splendor,
life in an up-thrust, thick-moated tower.

She wept at the woodcutter's death,
but dug the grave herself, the same day.

She never went back. She didn't need to.
Birds flittered over the new grass, the moles hummed.

AILEEN FISHER

Cinderella Grass

Overnight the new green grass
turned to Cinderella glass.

Frozen rain decked twigs and weeds
with strings of Cinderella beads.

Glassy slippers, trim and neat,
covered all the clover's feet . . .
just as if there'd been a ball
with a magic wand and all.

VII. LITTLE RED RIDING HOOD

JAMES WHITCOMB RILEY

Maymie's Story of Red Riding-Hood

W'y, one time wuz a little-weenty dirl,
An' she wuz named Red Riding-Hood, 'cause her—
Her *Ma* she maked a little red cloak fer her
'At turnt up over her head.—An' it uz all
Ist one piece o' red cardinul 'at's like
The drate-long stockin's the storekeepers has.—
Oh! it 'uz purtiest cloak in all the world
An' *all* this town er anywheres they is!
An' so, one day, her Ma she put it on
Red Riding-Hood, she did—one day, she did—
An' it 'uz *Sund'y*—'cause the little cloak
It 'uz too nice to wear ist *ever'* day
An' *all* the time!—An' so her Ma, she put
It on Red Riding-Hood—an' telled her not
To dit no dirt on it ner dit it mussed
Ner nothin'! An'—an'—nen her Ma she dot
Her little basket out, 'at Old Kriss bringed
Her wunst—one time, he did. An' nen she fill'
It full o' whole lots an' 'bundance o' dood things t' eat
(Allus my Dran'ma *she* says "bundance,' too.)
An' so her Ma fill' little Red Riding-Hood's
Nice basket all ist full o' dood things t' eat,
An' tell her take 'em to her old Dran'ma—
An' not to *spill* 'em, neever—'cause ef she
'Ud stump her toe an' spill 'em, her Dran'ma
She'll haf to *punish* her!

An' nen—An' so
Little Red Riding-Hood she p'omised she
'Ud be all careful nen, an' cross' her heart
'At she won't run an' spill 'em all fer six—
Five—ten—two-hundred-bushel-dollars-gold!
An' nen she kiss' her Ma doo'-by an' went
A-skippin' off—away fur off frough the
Big woods, where her Dran'ma she live at—
No!—
She didn't do *a-skippin'*, like I said:—
She ist went *walkin'*—careful-like an' slow—

Ist like a little lady—walkin' 'long
As all polite an' nice—an' slow—an' straight—
An' turn her toes—ist like she's marchin' in
The Sund'y-School k-session!

An'—an'—so
She 'uz a-doin' along—an' doin' along—
On frough the drate-big woods—'cause her Dran'ma
She live 'way, 'way fur off frough the big woods
From *her* Ma's house. So when Red Riding-Hood
Dit to do there, she allus have most fun—
When she do frough the drate-big woods, you know.—
'Cause she ain't feard a bit o' anything!
An' so she sees the little hoppty-birds
'At's in the trees, an' flyin' all around,
An' singin' dlad as ef their parunts said
They'll take 'em to the magic-lantern show!
An' she 'ud pull the purty flowers an' things
A-growin' round the stumps.—An' she 'ud ketch
The purty butterflies, an' drasshoppers,
An' stick pins frough 'em—No!—I ist *said* that!—
'Cause she's too dood an' kind an 'bedient
To *hurt* things thataway.—She'd *ketch* 'em, though,
An' ist *play* wiv 'em ist a little while,
An' nen she'd let 'em fly away, she would,
An' ist skip on ad'in to her Dran'ma's.

An' so, while she 'uz doin' 'long an' 'long,
First thing you know they 'uz a drate-big old
Mean wicked Wolf jumped out 'at wanted t' eat
Her up, but *dassent* to—'cause wite clos't there
They wuz a Man a-choppin' wood, an' you
Could *hear* him.—So the old Wolf he 'uz *feard*
Only to ist be *kind* to her.—So he
Ist 'tended-like he wuz dood friends to her
An' says, "Dood morning, little Red Riding-Hood!"—
All ist as kind!

An' nen Riding-Hood
She say "Dood morning," too—all kind an' nice—
Ist like her Ma she learn'—No!—mustn't say
"Learn'," 'cause *"learn'"* it's unproper.—So she say
It like her *Ma* she *"teached"* her.—An'—so she
Ist says "Dood morning" to the Wolf—'cause she
Don't know ut-tall 'at he's a *wicked* Wolf
An' want to eat her up!
Nen old Wolf smile
An' say, so kind: "Where air you doin' at?"
Nen little Red Riding-Hood she say: "I'm doin'
To my Dran'ma's, 'cause my Ma say I might."
Nen, when she tell him that, the old Wolf he
Ist turn an' light out frough the big thick woods,
Where she can't see him any more. An' so
She think he's went to *his* house—but he hain't,—
He's went to her Dran'ma's, to be there first—
An' *ketch* her, ef she don't watch mighty sharp
What she's about!
An' nen when the old Wolf
Dit to her Dran'ma's house, he's purty smart,—
An' so he 'tend-like *he's* Red Riding-Hood,
An' knock at th' door. An' Riding-Hood's Dran'ma
She's sick in bed an' can't come to the door
An' open it. So th' old Wolf knock' *two* times.
An' nen Red Riding-Hood's Dran'ma she says,
"Who's there?" she says. An' old Wolf 'tends-like he's
Little Red Riding-Hood, you know, an' make'
His voice soun' ist like hers, an' says: "It's me,
Dran'ma—an' I'm Red Riding-Hood an' I'm
Ist come to *see* you."
Nen her old Dran'ma
She think it *is* little Red Riding-Hood,
An' so she say: "Well, come in nen an' make
You'se'f at home," she says, " 'cause I'm down sick
In bed, an' got the 'ralgia, so's I can't
Dit up an' let ye in."

An' so th' old Wolf
Ist march' in nen an' shet the door ad'in,
An' *drowl'*, he did, an' *splunge'* up on the bed
An' et up old Miz Riding-Hood 'fore she
Could put her specs on an' see who it wuz.—
An' so she never knowed *who* et her up!

An' nen the wicked Wolf he ist put on
Her nightcap, an' all covered up in bed—
Like he wuz *her*, you know.
Nen, purty soon
Here come along little Red Riding-Hood,
An' *she* knock' at the door. An' old Wolf 'tend-
Like *he's* her Dran'ma; an' he say, "Who's there?"
Ist like her Dran'ma say, you know. An' so
Little Red Riding-Hood she say: "It's *me*,
Dran'ma—an' I'm Red Riding-Hood an' I'm
Ist come to *see* you."
An' nen old Wolf nen
He cough an' say: "Well, come in nen an' make
You'se'f at home," he says, "'cause I'm down sick
In bed, an' got the 'ralgia, so's I can't
Dit up an' let ye in."
An' so she think
It's her Dran'ma a-talkin'.—So she ist
Open' the door an' come in, an' set down
Her basket, an' taked off her things, an' bringed
A chair an' clumbed up on the bed, wite by
The old big Wolf she thinks is her Dran'ma—
Only she thinks the old Wolf's dot whole lots
More bigger ears, an' lots more whiskers, too,
Than her Dran'ma; an' so Red Riding-Hood
She's kind o' skeered a little. So she says,
"Oh, Dran'ma, what *big eyes* you dot!" An' nen
The old Wolf says: "They're ist big thataway
'Cause I'm so dlad to see you!"

Nen she says,
"Oh, Dran'ma, what a drate-big nose you dot!"
Nen th' old Wolf says: "It's ist big thataway
Ist 'cause I smell the dood things 'at you bringed
Me in the basket!"

An' nen Riding-Hood
She says, "Oh-me-oh-*my*! Dran'ma! what big
White long sharp teeth you dot!"

Nen old Wolf says:
"Yes—an' they're thataway"—an' drowled—
"They're thataway," he says, "to *eat* you wiv!"
An nen he ist *jump'* at her.—

But she *scream'*—
An' *scream'*, she did.—So's 'at the Man
'At wuz a-choppin' wood, you know,—*he* hear,
An' come a-runnin' in there wiv his ax;
An', 'fore the old Wolf know' what he's about,
He split his old brains out an' killed him s' quick
It make' his head swim!—An' Red Riding-Hood
She wuzn't hurt at all!

An' the big Man
He tooked her all safe home, he did, an' tell
Her Ma she's all right an' ain't hurt at all
An' old Wolf's dead an' killed—an' ever'thing!—
So her Ma wuz so tickled an' so proud,
She gived *him* all the good things t' eat they wuz
'At's in the basket, an' she tell' him 'at
She's much oblige', an' say to "call ad'in."
An' story's honest *truth*—an' all *so*, too!

GUY WETMORE CARRYL

Red Riding Hood

Most worthy of praise were the virtuous ways
Of Little Red Riding Hood's ma,
And no one was ever more cautious and clever
Than Little Red Riding Hood's pa.
They never misled, for they meant what they said,
And frequently said what they meant:
They were careful to show her the way she should go,
And the way that they showed her she went.
For obedience she was effusively thanked,
And for anything else she was carefully spanked.

It thus isn't strange that Red Riding Hood's range
Of virtues so steadily grew,
That soon she won prizes of various sizes,
And golden encomiums too.
As a general rule she was head of her school,
And at six was so notably smart
That they gave her a check for reciting The Wreck
Of the Hesperus wholly by heart.
And you all will applaud her the more, I am sure,
When I add that the money she gave to the poor.

At eleven this lass had a Sunday-school class,
At twelve wrote a volume of verse,
At fourteen was yearning for glory, and learning
To be a professional nurse.
To a glorious height the young paragon might
Have climbed, if not nipped in the bud,
But the following year struck her smiling career
With a dull and a sickening thud!
(I have shed a great tear at the thought of her pain,
And must copy my manuscript over again!)

Not dreaming of harm, one day on her arm
A basket she hung. It was filled
With drinks made of spices, and jellies, and ices,
And chicken-wings, carefully grilled,
And a savory stew, and a novel or two
She persuaded a neighbor to loan,

And a Japanese fan, and a hot-water can,
And a bottle of eau de cologne,
And the rest of the things that your family fill
Your room with whenever you chance to be ill.

She expected to find her decrepit but kind
Old grandmother waiting her call,
Exceedingly ill. Oh, that face on the pillow
Did not look familiar at all!
With a whitening cheek she started to speak,
But her peril she instantly saw:
Her grandma had fled and she'd tackled instead
Four merciless paws and a maw!
When the neighbors came running the wolf to subdue,
He was licking his chops—and Red Riding Hood's, too!

At this terrible tale some readers will pale,
And others with horror grow dumb,
And yet it was better, I fear, he should get her:—
Just think what she might have become!
For an infant so keen might in future have been
A woman of awful renown,
Who carried on fights for her feminine rights,
As the Mayor of an Arkansas town,
Or she might have continued the sins of her 'teens
And come to write verse for the Big Magazines!

THE MORAL: There's nothing much glummer
Than children whose talents appal.
One much prefers those that are dumber.
And as for the paragons small—
If a swallow cannot make a summer,
It can bring on a summary fall!

A. D. HOPE

Coup de Grâce

Just at that moment the Wolf,
Shag jaws and slavering grin,
Steps from the property wood.
O, what a gorge, what a gulf
Opens to gobble her in.
Little Red Riding Hood!

O, what a face full of fangs!
Eyes like saucers at least
Roll to seduce and beguile.
Miss, with her dimples and bangs,
Thinks him a handsome beast;
Flashes the Riding Hood Smile;

Stands her ground like a queen,
Velvet red of the rose
Framing each little milk-tooth,
Pink tongue peeping between.
Then, wider than anyone knows,
Opens her minikin mouth,

Swallows up Wolf in a trice;
Tail going down gives a flick,
Caught as she closes her jaws.
Bows, all sugar and spice.
O, what a lady-like trick!
O, what a round of applause!

ANNE SEXTON

Little Red Riding Hood

Many are the deceivers:

The suburban matron,
proper in the supermarket,
list in hand so she won't suddenly fly,
buying her Duz and Chuck Wagon dog food,
meanwhile ascending from earth,
letting her stomach fill up with helium,
letting her arms go loose as kite tails,
getting ready to meet her lover
a mile down Apple Crest Road
in the Congregational Church parking lot.

Two seemingly respectable women
come up to an old Jenny
and show her an envelope
full of money
and promise to share the booty
if she'll give them ten thou
as an act of faith.
Her life savings are under the mattress
covered with rust stains
and counting.
They are as wrinkled as prunes
but negotiable.
The two women take the money and disappear.
Where is the moral?
Not all knives are for
stabbing the exposed belly.
Rock climbs on rock
and it only makes a seashore.
Old Jenny has lost her belief in mattresses
and now she has no wastebasket in which
to keep her youth.

The standup comic
on the "Tonight" show
who imitates the Vice President
and cracks up Johnny Carson

and delays sleep for millions
of bedfellows watching between their feet,
slits his wrist the next morning
in the Algonquin's old-fashioned bathroom,
the razor in his hand like a toothbrush,
wall as anonymous as a urinal,
the shower curtain his slack rubberman audience,
and then the slash
as simple as opening a letter
and the warm blood breaking out like a rose
upon the bathtub with its claw and ball feet.

And I. I too.
Quite collected at cocktail parties,
meanwhile in my head
I'm undergoing open-heart surgery.
The heart, poor fellow,
pounding on his little tin drum
with a faint death beat.
The heart, that eyeless beetle,
enormous that Kafka beetle,
running panicked through his maze,
never stopping one foot after the other
one hour after the other
until he gags on an apple
and it's all over.

And I. I too again.
I built a summer house on Cape Ann.
A simple A-frame and this too was
a deception—nothing haunts a new house.
When I moved in with a bathing suit and tea bags
the ocean rumbled like a train backing up
and at each window secrets came in
like gas. My mother, that departed soul,
sat in my Eames chair and reproached me
for losing her keys to the old cottage.
Even in the electric kitchen there was
the smell of a journey. The ocean

was seeping through its frontiers
and laying me out on its wet rails.
The bed was stale with my childhood
and I could not move to another city
where the worthy make a new life.

Long ago
there was a strange deception:
a wolf dressed in frills,
a kind of transvestite.
But I get ahead of my story.
In the beginning
there was just little Red Riding Hood,
so called because her grandmother
made her a red cape and she was never without it.
It was her Linus blanket, besides
it was red, as red as the Swiss flag,
yes it was red, as red as chicken blood.
But more than she loved her riding hood
she loved her grandmother who lived
far from the city in the big wood.

This one day her mother gave her
a basket of wine and cake
to take to her grandmother
because she was ill.
Wine and cake?
Where's the aspirin? The penicillin?
Where's the fruit juice?
Peter Rabbit got camomile tea.
But wine and cake it was.

On her way in the big wood
Red Riding Hood met the wolf.
Good day, Mr. Wolf, she said,
thinking him no more dangerous
than a streetcar or a panhandler.
He asked where she was going
and she obligingly told him.

There among the roots and trunks
with the mushrooms pulsing inside the moss
he planned how to eat them both,
the grandmother an old carrot
and the child a shy budkin
in a red red hood.
He bade her to look at the bloodroot,
the small bunchberry and the dogtooth
and pick some for her grandmother.
And this she did.
Meanwhile he scampered off
to Grandmother's house and ate her up
as quick as a slap.
Then he put on her nightdress and cap
and snuggled down into the bed.
A deceptive fellow.

Red Riding Hood
knocked on the door and entered
with her flowers, her cake, her wine.
Grandmother looked strange,
a dark and hairy disease it seemed.
Oh Grandmother, what big ears you have,
ears, eyes, hands and then the teeth.
The better to eat you with, my dear.
So the wolf gobbled Red Riding Hood down
like a gumdrop. Now he was fat.
He appeared to be in his ninth month
and Red Riding Hood and her grandmother
rode like two Jonahs up and down with
his every breath. One pigeon. One partridge.

He was fast asleep,
dreaming in his cap and gown,
wolfless.
Along came a huntsman who heard
the loud contented snores
and knew that was no grandmother.
He opened the door and said,

So it's you, old sinner.
He raised his gun to shoot him
when it occurred to him that maybe
the wolf had eaten up the old lady.
So he took a knife and began cutting open
the sleeping wolf, a kind of caesarian section.

It was a carnal knife that let
Red Riding Hood out like a poppy,
quite alive from the kingdom of the belly.
And grandmother too
still waiting for cakes and wine.
The wolf, they decided, was too mean
to be simply shot so they filled his belly
with large stones and sewed him up.
He was as heavy as a cemetery
and when he woke up and tried to run off
he fell over dead. Killed by his own weight.
Many a deception ends on such a note.

The huntsman and the grandmother and Red Riding
  Hood
sat down by his corpse and had a meal of wine and
  cake.
Those two remembering
nothing naked and brutal
from that little death,
that little birth,
from their going down
and their lifting up.

VITOMIL ZUPAN

A Fairy Tale

I saw a very strange fairy tale.
Somebody fell in love with somebody.
It was obvious that there must come to an action,
quickly and effectively.
They let out the blood-hounds. Good hounds. Well
looking
hounds. Well educated hounds.
Good officials followed them. Not so well looking. Still
well trained.
After them went the coroners
in a good wagon.
And then the wolf swallowed the gran'ma
The Red-cap had an accident on a cross-way
a pitcher of milk fell on the floor
and the hounds began to lick it.
The officials began to beat the hounds
the coroners went for a drink
and somebody escaped with HER.
What a nice fairy tale indeed.

MYRA SKLAREW

Red Riding Hood at the Acropolis

kakó kakó said grandmother
concerning the wolf
o giorgos old man
what sharp teeth you have
she said as they rounded the bend
between skylla and charybdis
what big ears

but the old wolf
was by then
strapped to his mast
it rose up through him
like his furry soul
he was thinking of return
of the way the sun
lay in wait in the forest
he was thinking of a ritual
in which an old woman
a tender girl
and a hunter
would play their parts

without him
even the sea
would come apart
even this story
so he would go on blindly
as wolf as old man
and they would be born
out of his belly
like elpenor
in the land of the dead
over the pit
where the dark clouding blood
runs in

or like aphrodite
the first time she stood
on her shell coming out of the sea
long have I sought you
said the hunter
as he cut open the sleeping wolf

how dark inside a wolf
said little red riding hood
springing forth

kakó kakó said grandmother
still wearing her ancient
polka dot dress

(kakó—Gr. bad, evil)

OLGA BROUMAS

Little Red Riding Hood

I grow old, old
without you, Mother, landscape
of my heart. No child, no daughter between my bones
has moved, and passed
out screaming, dressed in her mantle of blood

as I did
once through your pelvic scaffold, stretching it
like a wishbone, your tenderest skin
strung on its bow and tightened
against the pain. I slipped out like an arrow, but not
before

the midwife
plunged to her wrist and guided
my baffled head to its first mark. High forceps
might, in that one instant, have accomplished
what you and that good woman failed
in all these years to do: cramp
me between the temples, hobble
my baby feet. Dressed in my red hood, howling, I
went—

evading
the white-clad doctor and his fancy claims: microscope,
stethoscope, scalpel, all
the better to see with, to hear,
and to eat—straight from your hollowed basket
into the midwife's skirts. I grew up

good at evading, and when you said,
"Stick to the road and forget the flowers, there's
wolves in those bushes, mind
where you got to go, mind
you get there," I
minded. I kept

to the road, kept
the hood secret, kept what it sheathed more
secret still. I opened
it only at night, and with other women
who might be walking the same road to their own
grandma's house, each with her basket of gifts, her
 small hood
safe in the same part. I minded well. I have no daughter

to trace that road, back to your lap with my laden
basket of love. I'm growing
old, old
without you. Mother, landscape
of my heart, architect of my body, what other gesture
can I conceive

to make with it
that would reach you, alone
in your house and waiting, across this improbable forest
peopled with wolves and our lost, flower-gathering
sisters they feed on.

ROALD DAHL

Little Red Riding Hood and the Wolf

As soon as Wolf began to feel
That he would like a decent meal,
He went and knocked on Grandma's door.
When Grandma opened it, she saw
The sharp white teeth, the horrid grin,
And Wolfie said, "May I come in?"
Poor Grandmamma was terrified,
"He's going to eat me up!" she cried.
And she was absolutely right.
He ate her up in one big bite.
But Grandmamma was small and tough,
And Wolfie wailed, "That's not enough!
I haven't yet begun to feel
That I have had a decent meal!"
He ran around the kitchen yelping,
"I've *got* to have a second helping!"
Then added with a frightful leer,
"I'm therefore going to wait right here
Till Little Miss Red Riding Hood
Comes home from walking in the wood."
He quickly put on Grandma's clothes,
(Of course he hadn't eaten those).
He dressed himself in coat and hat.
He put on shoes and after that
He even brushed and curled his hair,
Then sat himself in Grandma's chair.
In came the little girl in red.
She stopped. She stared. And then she said,

"What great big ears you have, Grandma."
"All the better to hear you with," the Wolf replied.
"What great big eyes you have, Grandma,"
said Little Red Riding Hood.
"All the better to see you with," the Wolf replied.

He sat there watching her and smiled.
He thought, I'm going to eat this child.
Compared with her old Grandmamma
She's going to taste like caviar.

Then Little Red Riding Hood said, *"But Grandma, what a lovely great big furry coat you have on."*

"That's wrong!" cried Wolf. "Have you forgot
To tell me what BIG TEETH I've got?
Ah well, no matter what you say,
I'm going to eat you anyway."
The small girl smiles. One eyelid flickers.
She whips a pistol from her knickers.
She aims it at the creature's head
And *bang bang bang*, she shoots him dead.
A few weeks later, in the wood,
I came across Miss Riding Hood.
But what a change! No cloak of red,
No silly hood upon her head.
She said, "Hello, and do please note
My lovely furry wolfskin coat."

VIII. SLEEPING BEAUTY

WALTER DE LA MARE

Sleeping Beauty

The scent of bramble fills the air,
Amid her folded sheets she lies,
The gold of evening in her hair,
The blue of morn shut in her eyes.

How many a changing moon hath lit
The unchanging roses of her face!
Her mirror ever broods on it
In silver stillness of the days.

Oft flits the moth on filmy wings
Into his solitary lair;
Shrill evensong the cricket sings
From some still shadow in her hair.

In heat, in snow, in wind, in flood,
She sleeps in lovely loneliness,
Half-folded like an April bud
On winter-haunted trees.

WILFRED OWEN

The Sleeping Beauty

Sojourning through a southern realm in youth,
I came upon a house by happy chance
Where bode a marvellous Beauty. There, romance
Flew faerily until I lit on truth—
For lo! the fair Child slumbered. Though, forsooth,
She lay not blanketed in drowsy trance,
But leapt alert of limb and keen of glance,
From sun to shower; from gaiety to ruth;
Yet breathed her loveliness asleep in her:
For, when I kissed, her eyelids knew no stir.
So back I drew tiptoe from that Princess,
Because it was too soon, and not my part,
To start voluptuous pulses in her heart,
And kiss her to the world of Consciousness.

JAMES WHITCOMB RILEY

A Sleeping Beauty

I

An alien wind that blew and blew
Over the fields where the ripe grain grew,

Sending ripples of shine and shade
That crept and crouched at her feet and played.

The sea-like summer washed the moss
Till the sun-drenched lilies hung like floss,

Draping the throne of green and gold
That lulled her there like a queen of old.

II

Was it the hum of a bumblebee,
Or the long-hushed bugle eerily

Winding a call to the daring Prince
Lost in the wood long ages since?—

A dim old wood, with a palace rare
Hidden away in its depths somewhere!

Was it the Princess, tranced in sleep,
Awaiting her lover's touch to leap

Into the arms that bent above?—
To thaw his heart with the breath of love—

And cloy his lips, through her waking tears,
With the dead-ripe kiss of a hundred years!

III

An alien wind that blew and blew.—
I had blurred my eyes as the artists do,

Coaxing life to a half-sketched face,
Or dreaming bloom for a grassy place.

The bee droned on in an undertone;
And a shadow-bird trailed all alone

Across the wheat, while a liquid cry
Dripped from above, as it went by.

What to her was the far-off whir
Of the quail's quick wing or the chipmunk's
  chirr?—

What to her was the shade that slid
Over the hill where the reapers hid?—

Or what the hunter, with one foot raised,
As he turned to go—yet, pausing, gazed?

ELINOR WYLIE

Sleeping Beauty

Imprisoned in the marble block
Lies Beauty; granite is her dress;
The strong may carve from living rock
A lady like a lioness.

With hammer blow and chisel cut
They make the angry Beauty leap.
For me the obdurate stone is shut;
How shall I wake her from her sleep?

An acorn tossed against an oak,
A hazel wand that turns—and look!
She parts the leaves, a pearly smoke,
She cleaves the earth—a silver brook.

EVELYN M. WATSON

A Sleeping Beauty

What dainty world is yours, in which you sleep,
A gentle realm of roses, dew, and song,
Of fragrances that drift and slowly sweep
In some broad bounding current, far along
Until you chance upon the scent of wines,
The nectars of a thousand garden blows,
And in that current with its swift designs
You find your Princess in her first repose.
And do you dream of her, your living queen,
The leagues you'd wing to her so happily
By glades and glens and meadows sweetly green
To find her on some spread acacia tree?
Are you the one among her multitude,
(Or just another pair of brilliant wings)—
Take you the Nuptial Flight in solitude
To serve the God of all triumphant things?

You sleep tonight without a troubled stir,
So undismayed about your life's true quest
So undisturbed, my lovely wanderer,
You give new values to my thoughts of Rest.

ROBERT S. HILLYER

And When the Prince Came

May the castle lie in slumber
For another thousand years,
Beldame fallen by her spindle,
Sentries full-length by their spears.
Sleeping hands no toil shall cumber,
Sleeping hearts no love shall kindle,
Sleeping eyes are void of tears.

May the blue flame in the hallways
Burn like tapers by the dead,
May no clarion of duty
Rouse the old King from his bed.
And the Princess, may she always
Lie in peace, for Sleeping Beauty
Blossoms only to be shed.

In my vision I had bound her
To my fate, a mortal wife
Wakened from a sleep immortal
By the urgent kiss of life.
But I left her as I found her
And above the southern portal
This I lettered with my knife:

"Loves there are that feast in giving;
Slumber still—my love was such;
Bonds that strengthen as they sever,
Lips that pause and will not touch.
Sleep, Beloved, safe from living;
Sleep, Beloved, safe for ever
From the one who loved too much."

RANDALL JARRELL

The Sleeping Beauty: Variation of the Prince

After the thorns I came to the first page.
He lay there gray in his fur of dust:
As I bent to open an eye, I sneezed.
But the ball looked by me, blue
As the sky it stared into . . .
And the sentry's cuirass is red with rust.

Children play inside: the dirty hand
Of the little mother, an inch from the child
That has worn out, burst, and blown away,
Uncurling to it—does not uncurl.
The bloom on the nap of their world
Is set with thousands of dawns of dew.

But at last, at the center of all the webs
Of the realm established in your blood,
I find you; and—look!—the drop of blood
Is there still, under the dust of your finger:
I force it, slowly, down from your finger
And it falls and rolls away, as it should.

And I bend to touch (just under the dust
That was roses once) the steady lips
Parted between a breath and a breath
In love, for the kiss of the hunger, Death.
Then I stretch myself beside you, lay
Between us, there in the dust, His sword.

When the world ends—it will never end—
The dust at last will fall from your eyes
In judgment, and I shall whisper:
"For hundreds of thousands of years I have slept
Beside you, here in the last long world
That you had found; that I have kept."

When they come for us—no one will ever come—
I shall stir from my long light sleep,
I shall whisper, "Wait, wait! . . . She is asleep."
I shall whisper, gazing, up to the gaze of the hunter,
Death, and close with the tips of the dust of my hand
The lids of the steady—
                                                  Look, He is fast asleep!

MARY HUTTON

The Sleeping Beauty

Tell me, is there among you one
all gertrude of paralysis,
though the door strikes down her five raised knuckles,
knocks?

Where is the singular, the one,
of plural ghost the graduated eye,
unique of stem, who sleeps within her sleep,
and turns within his arms her bladewide smile?

Ah, what did I kill once? Where? What hide?
Hide from myself?
All talent, love and memory conceal
so that I lie here still
and no sound comes,
though dark between heavy briars
the hedge burns like a crown?

O my incurable,
of love they say,
as in some times of solid still
when all the grass is shut off and the trees,
those groves of ocelots,
dissolved,
their corners flowing,
who has not
bent, and in his love's dark mouth,
found himself upon a road before a darkened house,
its fences full of wars,
and all its hundred years of roses stopped?
Knocked and heard no knock unfasten from his
knuckles?

E. L. MAYO

The Sleeping Beauty

In a place where hunchbacks and old women
Quarreled in their thin voices all the day
This temporizing grew intolerable:
I knew that here the Sleeping Beauty lay.

(Had they known it all the time and been
Sly servitors where I could only seize
Bad temper and distorted images?)
Sight ended the old argument. I saw

Her tower clear against the star-picked blue
Over their hovels. It was no affair
Of a cloud and the moon's subtle conjunction; thorns
Hatched me all criss-cross as I hacked my way through

And stumbled bloody still and breathing still
Into a country where no footsteps fall
And where from moat, to keep, to citadel
Spider-webs lie like water.

I silvered as I entered through the door
Where time cannot prevail
But howls outside forever where I found her
Asleep, beautiful, the cobwebs round her.

LEONARD COHEN

The Sleeping Beauty

"You are brave," I told the Sleeping Beauty,
"to climb these steps into my home,
but I regret your man, the Kissing Prince, is gone."
"You don't understand what story I am from," she said,
"we both know who lives in this garden."
Still, all those following nights
she never knew to call me Beast or Swan.

ARTHUR FREEMAN

Beauty, Sleeping

My mistress' inmost heart,
how does it keep so deep
that neither sentiment nor art
can sound its sleep?

Where does this dreamer lie
when the prince rides round the camp?
Up in some tower, high and dry,
or deep and damp?

Is it a citadel
he must perforce assail,
or is it woods, or might he as well
begin in jail?

And when he knows, then what?
Suppose there is a lock,
and the last doors are bolted shut—
shall he knock?

Grant him a miracle.
Admit him to the place,
and let him bend to break the spell,
facing her face,

And then, ironic Three,
administer your pill—
let him embrace her perfectly
and her sleep still.

Oh mistress mine, I fear
I seek who shall refuse me.
You who are difficult and dear—
excuse me.

SARA HENDERSON HAY

The Sleeper

1

(She speaks . . .)
I wish the Prince had left me where he found me,
Wrapped in a rosy trance so charmed and deep
I might have lain a hundred years asleep.
I hate this new and noisy world around me!
The palace hums with sightseers from town,
There's not a quiet spot that I can find.
And, worst of all, he's chopped the brambles down—
The lovely briars I've felt so safe behind.

But if he thinks that with a kiss or two
He'll buy my dearest privacy, or shake me
Out of the cloistered world I've loved so long,
Or tear the pattern of my dream, he's wrong.
Nothing this clumsy trespasser can do
Will ever touch my heart, or really wake me.

2

(He speaks . . .)

I used to think that slumbrous look she wore,
The dreaming air, the drowsy-lidded eyes,
Were artless affectation, nothing more.
But now, and far too late, I realize
How sound she sleeps, behind a thorny wall
Of rooted selfishness, whose stubborn strands
I broke through once, to kiss her lips and hands,
And wake her heart, that never woke at all.

I wish I'd gone away that self-same hour,
Before I learned how, like her twining roses,
She bends to her own soft, implacable uses
The pretty tactics that such vines employ,
To hide the poisoned barb beneath the flower,
To cling about, to strangle, to destroy.

JOAN SWIFT

Vancouver Island

That dark form lies in a cumulus tower,
Sleeping Beauty.
A shiver of rain pricks her,
The fog unwinds its spindle.
Old Crone South Wind weaves her an evil weather.
Behind gray walls she dreams a hundred years.
Tatoosh, your lighthouse is no prince—
Her coves' blue delicate fingers fold beyond your spear.

Slip Point, do hills heave out of their spell
At your call?
She's in another country.

But remember the fairy tale.
Late afternoon,
When the sky seems most a thicket
And clouds put thorns in the sea,
The Sun comes streaking, the gold-armored Sun,
To kiss her green hills and lavender beaches—
Is it into, or out of, illusion?

DOUGLAS KNIGHT

Sleeping Beauty: August

For now the whetting of mind has stopped,
Bright sparks of memory quiet on the floor,
And even the leather honing of scholars stilled.
The trees are burdened with summer; casual thunder
Fails to disrupt the rhythm of cloud and wind
(Which we did not invent, but only admire).
Each tower is rigid, while the mythic castle
Of August swims in our enchanted air,
Holding all that we failed to do and did,
All that we dreamed, and will enact again
When young September breaks the magic spell
And sends us back to books, ambition, people.

SARA DE FORD

The Sleeping Beauty

In your scarred, peeling crib you lay neglected,
Twisting the patched and cast-off sheet
Your older sisters wore threadbare. And while
You screamed yourself red-faced, the sweet
Soft-handed fairies followed them, to smile
On gifts their love selected:
Goodness for Mary, quick bright wit for Grace,
A dower of wealth, long life, and love for each,
Till there were no gifts left for you to reach
Your square coarse hands to grasp. No trifle lay
   rejected.

Then the sly witch, malignant, dared to chatter
Her spell: the spindle prick of sex,
To doom you stuporous, with only deep
Breath stirring a gross weight, to vex
Life with this paralyzing death of sleep,
Inert and brutal matter.
So now, grown old, you sleep. The keen wound festers
In rancid sores that slaver, crust, and break;
Your castle lies enthralled; no one can wake
The torpid consciousness, the trance no sound can
   shatter.

CHARLES JOHNSON

Sleeping Beauty

A Beautiful Black man
Sleeping in a corner
His mind wandering into the deepest of
Darkness
His suffering eyes closed
His mouth open wide as if he
Wants to eat up the White world
And spit it out into the hand
of the White man and then
wake up.

HOWARD NEMEROV

Sleeping Beauty

They told me this story a long time ago,
When I was a child, to make me go to sleep.
I never should have been surprised,
But then, being young, I could not know they meant
My eyes to be the ones that closed
When the time came and the clock struck
And the dream was tolled by the steeple bell.

I listen to the castle sleep, the grooms
In the stables, courtiers on the marble floors,
The scratch of dust descending and the rose
Thickets breaking forth flowers and thorns;
And I ask in sleep, is this my sleep?
Am I the one the wide world cannot find
Nor even the prince in the forest foresee?

This ends only with a kiss, the story said.
Then all the snoring barons will arise
And the dogs begin to bark, the king and queen
Order their coach and four—all on a kiss
The whole world will begin to happen again,
People will yawn, stretch, begin to forget
Whatever they dreamed that was so like a dream.

And shall I also, with the kiss, forget
That I was the one who dreamed them all,
Courtier and king, scullion and cook,
Horse in the stable and fly on the wall?
Forget the petals' whisper when they drift
Down where the untold princes die in blood
Because I dreamed the thicket and the thorn?

MAXINE KUMIN

The Archaeology of a Marriage

When Sleeping Beauty wakes up
she is almost fifty years old.
Time to start planning her retirement cottage.
The Prince in sneakers stands thwacking
his squash racquet. He plays
three nights a week at his club,
it gets the heart action up.
What *he* wants in the cottage
is a sauna and an extra-firm Beauty-
rest mattress, which *she* sees as an exquisite
sarcasm directed against her long slumber.
Was it *her* fault he took so long
to hack his way through the brambles?
Why didn't he carry a chainsaw
like any sensible woodsman?
Why, for that matter, should any
twentieth-century woman
have to lie down at the prick of
a spindle etcetera etcetera
and he is stung to reply
in kind and soon they are at it.

If only they could go back to
the simplest beginnings. She
remembers especially a snapshot
of herself in a checked gingham outfit.
He is wearing his Navy dress whites.
She remembers the illicit weekend
in El Paso, twenty years before
illicit weekends came out of the closet.
Just before Hiroshima
just before Nagasaki
they nervously straddled the border
he an ensign on a forged three-day pass
she a technical virgin from Boston.
What he remembers is vaster:
something about his whole future
compressed to a stolen weekend.
He was to be shipped out tomorrow

for the massive land intervention.
He was to have stormed Japan.
Then, merely thinking of dying
gave him a noble erection.

Now, thanatopsis is calmer,
the first ripe berry on the stem,
a loss leader luring his greedy
hands deeper into the thicket
than he has ever been.
Deeper than he cares to be.
At the sight of the castle, however,
he recovers his wits and backtracks
meanwhile picking. Soon his bucket
is heavier etcetera than ever
and he is older etcetera
and still no spell has been recast
back at Planned Acres Cottage.
Each day he goes forth to gather
small fruits. Each evening she stands
over the stewpot skimming
the acid foam from the jam
expecting to work things out
awaiting, you might say, a unicorn
her head stuffed full of old notions
and the slotted spoon in her hand.

JOHN DITSKY

Epithalamium

First a princess,
pricked, falls fast asleep,
her prince nearby. Thick ivy
grows upon the walls
& over windows;

their sleep is
cool & long, & no one
comes to set them free awake;
instead, their clock
tocks down,

then stops;
the princess & her
prince wake up to die; a house-
shaped mound of ivy
grows on dust.

LAURIE SHECK

Sleeping Beauty

A dark narrow stairway.
Each door we pass is chained
from inside; sometimes you hear the locks rattle
like the stirring of someone buried alive.

From her room you can see the lit windows,
each a golden cage
where the dark hands flutter and fall.

She wears a nightgown covered with roses.
It rests easily on her body
as if it had lain down to listen to her heart.

I don't know if her eyes see at all
as she stares at the tiled ceiling,
if she's counting the white squares.

When the man arrives she does not feel his kiss.
I want to tell her, *but that is not the story!*
you must wake up and love him!
Buses pass below the window, quietly as thieves.

The snow falling through the room is warm.
It is ashes in her hair, ashes
over her quiet face and hands.
It covers the windows, her eyes.

NOELLE CASKEY

Ripening

Sleeping Beauty without her hedge of thorns?
Impossible!

The prince must prick himself
once, twice, on the sharp spines
before he touches roses.

This is no evil wish.
It is a story.
All women sleep, some
for a hundred years.
The thorns

protect the dreaming rose
and spare unwary hunters
that blood-red wakening.

JANE SHORE

Sleeping Beauty

Green iridescent flies
are stuck like thumbtacks in the walls.
An enormous cauldron of water
begins boiling as the cook dozes
among the copper ladles—
hung like a row of shiny eighth notes on a staff.
The scullery maid's asleep on her feet.
Four ladies-in-waiting keep waiting
for their mistress to wake up.

Outside the palace walls,
the world works as before.
Scythes glint trails of crescent moons
below the wheat.
But acres west, within its white cocoon,
time contains another field
that sleep has struck like a flood.
This little red boat is a woman's skirt,
and notice how she floats in it,
but light floods the field, light
ignites the scarecrow's straw.
A farmer clutches a pitchfork
where a haystack has dissolved,
as if this oar
could steer him clear of the disaster.

Like sopranos in a Bach chorale,
the brambles spring up in unison.
In the attic, the princess sleeps
beside the wooden spindle.
One drop of blood embroiders her fingertip.
Whichever hour she wakes
will be morning.

Whatever face she wakes to
she will marry. In his bed
she will lie for the next twenty years.
But now, the child dreams her elegy
in the twilight passage before birth.
Her prince is moving closer.
In one minute he will kiss her.
Outside her window, behind the hive's
ungovernable hexagons, the queen bee stirs.

HAYDEN CARRUTH

Dornröschen

(The Sleeping Beauty)

Dornröschen, princess
      are not you too   held
In the crystalline moment of time stopped,
      you lying
So demurely propped,   naked and spelled,
On the couch of stone/
                              The purifying
Of icy fire surrounds you/
                                 Beyond it, quelled
Forever, is what might have been, for you,
      though the unimpelled,
Are the dreamer whose significant dreaming
Still brings,   dream by dream,   the seeming
That will be the world/
                              You lie in the center,
The integration
And the nowhereness of all things,
      as seasons of being are separated
      by a winter/
O northern princess,
                           see these apparitions,
How they gather in dreams, our history from the mist,
The meaningless, mysterious images of your dreaming
      reason
That you will know
                        the instant you are really kissed.

IX. SNOW WHITE

DONALD HALL

Mirror

"Mirror, mirror, on the wall,
Who is Donald Andrew Hall?"
"Self-knowledge is a rare disease.
These words, Donald, are vanity's."

SARA HENDERSON HAY

One of the Seven Has Somewhat to Say

Remember how it was before she came—?
The picks and shovels dropped beside the door,
The sink piled high, the meals any old time,
Our jackets where we'd flung them on the floor?
The mud tracked in, the clutter on the shelves.
None of us shaved, or more than halfway clean . . .
Just seven old bachelors, living by ourselves?
Those were the days, if you know what I mean.

She scrubs, she sweeps, she even dusts the ceilings:
She's made us build a tool shed for our stuff.
Dinner's at eight, the table setting's formal
And if I weren't afraid I'd hurt her feelings
I'd move, until we get her married off,
And things can gradually slip back to normal.

GERALD LOCKLIN

The Dwarf

She went away from us upon a snow-white
steed, the forest virgin scented with
the rain of evergreen, to while the mythic
hours in a prince's castle. Was it right

of her to take away her apple
innocence from seven dappled
dwarfs, to arbitrarily
absent us from felicity?

She went away to share a snow-white bed
with some tall aqua velva future king
who'll never know the pleasure wrested
from a woman willing yet unwilling,

nor how bigly bad a simple tree
appears to a tiny man, nor will they ever
either of them know the human thing
is not to be snow-white but to be ugly.

ROBERT M. CHUTE

Snow White

You say your fine, flatchested stepmother
bought a fattening funhouse mirror for her
wall? Crying "who's the bustiest of all?"
Then tried to feed your well fruited sister
a loaded pomme de terre? Now sister won't
undress while her husband's there? Always
holds her arms folded across her empty
maternity dress? I guess fairy tales

have gone to hell along with all fiction.
We used to think life real, stories, novels,
were conceits, toyfull inventions. Now we
find each fiction is unfinished, twisted,
but none-the-less a mirror for a life
that is less substantial than reflection.

ROBERT GILLESPIE

Snow White

She found herself 7 no less
dwarfs!
Such disney images—where did they come from, the
  yellow pages?—
grumpy sleepy sneezy happy dopey doc
Doc?
So why didn't she ever have any little dwarfs?
She was afraid of her father's handlebar moustache?
Who does she think she is, no hostility like the rest of us
toward stepmother? Her mother for dying?
What is really going on out there in that house in the
  woods?
Do they really know?
Does it ever get dirty and dull
fishy-stale in her innocent linens?
What are their little penises like, Snow White?
Does one finger
one lap another hump?
Does one sneeze? Unnatural
this absence of the natural. This division.
7 safe little men to father Mommy.
Why are they stay at homes?
Does she do the wash and cook casseroles or just be
  beautiful?
What was she *doing* out there in the wilderness in the
  first place,
looking for dwarfs?
Who made Snow White her big bed and cookies
letting her sit there and eat?
Home from their gold mine the swarthy dwarfs she
  inspires bring
bacon and mayonnaise. With love. They make spring
look like a dwarf.
Oh that lovely garden of a girl,
they stay because she takes their seed, because a
  garden stays.
They grow. Get roots down. Better men for it.

(And the apple woman and her uxorious
sidekick, what the fuck what a drag why not be the most
  beautiful
move on freak out kick *free*,
kicked out)
nibble nibble pick pick at the core of civilization
arch-fear proto-hate ur-guilt
their balls fall off like ripe peaches
pussy snow
beautiful sweet and kind and good.
Everybody agrees.
You soak me up, I'll cut you down;
because they soak her up. Because
they *like* it. Like looking up the blood-red and ebony
  snow
white they wish they came from.
Save us from our littleness
our ugliness without any beautiful touches
oh lift us up.
Now she is home, a king's son's wife, she is fairy tail
she eats roast beef with crackers
listening to the birds chirp
watching the snow melt
wondering where the brave woodcutter
where the men on white horse

ANNE SEXTON

Snow White and the Seven Dwarfs

No matter what life you lead
the virgin is a lovely number:
cheeks as fragile as cigarette paper,
arms and legs made of Limoges,
lips like Vin Du Rhône,
rolling her china-blue doll eyes
open and shut.
Open to say,
Good Day Mama,
and shut for the thrust
of the unicorn.
She is unsoiled.
She is as white as a bonefish.

Once there was a lovely virgin
called Snow White.
Say she was thirteen.
Her stepmother,
a beauty in her own right,
though eaten, of course, by age,
would hear of no beauty surpassing her own.
Beauty is a simple passion,
but, oh my friends, in the end
you will dance the fire dance in iron shoes.
The stepmother had a mirror to which she referred—
something like the weather forecast—
a mirror that proclaimed
the one beauty of the land.
She would ask,
Looking glass upon the wall,
who is fairest of us all?
And the mirror would reply,
You are fairest of us all.
Pride pumped in her like poison.

Suddenly one day the mirror replied,
Queen, you are full fair, 'tis true,
but Snow White is fairer than you.
Until that moment Snow White

had been no more important
than a dust mouse under the bed.
But now the queen saw brown spots on her hand
and four whiskers over her lip
so she condemned Snow White
to be hacked to death.
Bring me her heart, she said to the hunter,
and I will salt it and eat it.
The hunter, however, let his prisoner go
and brought a boar's heart back to the castle.
The queen chewed it up like a cube steak.
Now I am fairest, she said,
lapping her slim white fingers.

Snow White walked in the wildwood
for weeks and weeks.
At each turn there were twenty doorways
and at each stood a hungry wolf,
his tongue lolling out like a worm.
The birds called out lewdly,
talking like pink parrots,
and the snakes hung down in loops,
each a noose for her sweet white neck.
On the seventh week
she came to the seventh mountain
and there she found the dwarf house.
It was a droll as a honeymoon cottage
and completely equipped with
seven beds, seven chairs, seven forks
and seven chamber pots.
Snow White ate seven chicken livers
and lay down, at last, to sleep.

The dwarfs, those little hot dogs,
walked three times around Snow White,
the sleeping virgin. They were wise
and wattled like small czars.
Yes, It's a good omen,
they said, and will bring us luck.
They stood on tiptoe to watch
Snow White wake up. She told them
about the mirror and the killer-queen
and they asked her to stay and keep house.
Beware of your stepmother,
they said.
Soon she will know you are here.
While we are away in the mines
during the day, you must not
open the door.

Looking glass upon the wall . . .
The mirror told
and so the queen dressed herself in rags
and went out like a peddler to trap Snow White.
She went across seven mountains.
She came to the dwarf house
and Snow White opened the door
and bought a bit of lacing.
The queen fastened it tightly
around her bodice,
as tight as an Ace bandage,
so tight that Snow White swooned.
She lay on the floor, a plucked daisy.
When the dwarfs came home they undid the lace
and she revived miraculously.
She was as full of life as soda pop.
Beware of your stepmother,
they said.
She will try once more.

Looking glass upon the wall . . .
Once more the mirror told
and once more the queen dressed in rags
and once more Snow White opened the door.
This time she bought a poison comb,
a curved eight-inch scorpion,
and put it in her hair and swooned again.
The dwarfs returned and took out the comb
and she revived miraculously.
She opened her eyes as wide as Orphan Annie.
Beware, beware, they said,
but the mirror told,
the queen came,
Snow White, the dumb bunny,
opened the door
and she bit into a poison apple
and fell down for the final time.
When the dwarfs returned
they undid her bodice,
they looked for a comb,
but it did no good.
Though they washed her with wine
and rubbed her with butter
it was to no avail.
She lay as still as a gold piece.

The seven dwarfs could not bring themselves
to bury her in the black ground
so they made a glass coffin
and set it upon the seventh mountain
so that all who passed by
could peek in upon her beauty.
A prince came one June day
and would not budge.

He stayed so long his hair turned green
and still he would not leave.
The dwarfs took pity upon him
and gave him the glass Snow White—
its doll's eyes shut forever—
to keep in his far-off castle.
As the prince's men carried the coffin
they stumbled and dropped it
and the chunk of apple flew out
of her throat and she woke up miraculously.

And thus Snow White became the prince's bride.
The wicked queen was invited to the wedding feast
and when she arrived there were
red-hot iron shoes,
in the manner of red-hot roller skates,
clamped upon her feet.
First your toes will smoke
and then your heels will turn black
and you will fry upward like a frog,
she was told.
And so she danced until she was dead,
a subterranean figure,
her tongue flicking in and out
like a gas jet.
Meanwhile Snow White held court,
rolling her china-blue doll eyes open and shut
and sometimes referring to her mirror
as women do.

OLGA BROUMAS

Snow White

I could never want her (my mother)
until I myself had been wanted.
By a woman.

SUE SILVERMARIE

Three women
on a marriage bed, two
mothers and two daughters.
All through the war we slept
like this, grand-
mother, mother, daughter. Each night
between you, you pushed and pulled
me, willing
from warmth to warmth.

Later we fought so
bitterly through the peace
that father blanched in his uniform,
battlelined forehead milky
beneath the khaki brim.

We fought like mad-
women till the house-
hold shuddered, crockery fell, the bed-
clothes heaved in the only passion
they were, those maddening
peacetime years,
to know.

○

A woman
who loves a woman
who loves a woman
who loves a man.

If the circle
be unbroken . . .
Three years
into my marriage I woke with this
from an unspeakable dream
about you, fingers
electric, magnetized, repelling
my husband's flesh. Blond, clean,
miraculous, this alien
instrument I had learned to hone,
to prize, to pride myself on, instrument
for a music I couldn't dance,
cry or lose
anything to.
A curious
music, an un-
catalogued rhyme, mother / daughter, we lay
the both of us awake
that night you straddled
two continents and the wet
opulent ocean to visit us, bringing
your gifts.
Like two halves
of a two-colored apple—red
with discovery, green with fear—we lay
hugging the wall between us, whitewash
leaving its telltale tracks.
Already
some part of me had begun
the tally, dividing
the married spoils, claiming
your every gift.

○

Don't curse me, Mother, I couldn't bear
the bath
of your bitter spittle.

No salve
no ointment in a doctor's tube, no brew
in a witch's kettle, no lover's mouth, no friend
or god could heal me
if your heart
turned in anathema, grew stone
against me.
Defenseless
and naked as the day
I slid from you
twin voices keening and the cord
pulsing our common protest, I'm coming back
back to you
woman, flesh
of your woman's flesh, your fairest, most
faithful mirror,
my love
transversing me like a filament
wired to the noonday sun.

Receive
me, Mother.

o

o

ROALD DAHL

Snow White and the Seven Dwarfs

When little Snow White's mother died,
The king, her father, up and cried,
"Oh, what a nuisance! What a life!
Now I must find another wife!"
(It's never easy for a king
To find himself that sort of thing.)
He wrote to every magazine
And said, "I'm looking for a Queen."
At least ten thousand girls replied
And begged to be the royal bride.
The king said with a shifty smile,
"I'd like to give each one a trial."
However, in the end he chose
A lady called Miss Maclahose,
Who brought along a curious toy
That seemed to give her endless joy—
This was a mirror framed in brass,
A MAGIC TALKING LOOKING GLASS.
Ask it something day or night,
It always got the answer right.
For instance, if you were to say,
"Oh Mirror, what's for lunch today?"
The thing would answer in a trice,
"Today it's scrambled eggs and rice."
Now every day, week in, week out,
The spoiled and stupid Queen would shout,
"Oh Mirror Mirror on the wall,
Who is the fairest of them all?"
The Mirror answered every time,
"Oh Madam, you're the Queen sublime.
You are the only one to charm us,
Queen, you are the cat's pajamas."
For ten whole years the silly Queen
Repeated this absurd routine.
Then suddenly, one awful day
She heard the Magic Mirror say,
"From now on, Queen, you're *Number Two.*
Snow White is prettier than you!"
The Queen went absolutely wild.

She yelled, "I'm going to scrag that child!
I'll cook her flaming goose! I'll skin 'er!
I'll have her rotten guts for dinner!"
She called the Huntsman to her study.
She shouted at him, "Listen buddy!
You drag that filthy girl outside,
And see you take her for a ride!
Thereafter slit her ribs apart
And bring me back her bleeding heart!"
The Huntsman dragged the lovely child
Deep deep into the forest wild.
Fearing the worst, poor Snow White spake.
She cried, "Oh please give me a break!"
The knife was poised, the arm was strong.
She cried again, "I've done no *wrong*!"
The Huntsman's heart began to flutter.
It melted like a pound of butter.
He murmured, "Okay, beat it, kid,"
And you can bet your life she did.
Later, the Huntsman made a stop
Within the local butcher's shop,
And there he bought, for safety's sake,
A bullock's heart and one nice steak.
"Oh Majesty! Oh Queen!" he cried,
"That rotten little girl has died!
And just to prove I didn't cheat,
I've brought along these bits of meat."
The Queen cried out, "Bravissimo!
I trust you killed her nice and slow."
Then (this is the disgusting part)
The Queen sat down and ate the heart!
(I only hope she cooked it well.
Boiled heart can be as tough as hell.)
While all of this was going on,
Oh where, oh where had Snow White gone?
She'd found it easy, being pretty,
To hitch a ride into the city.
And there she'd got a job, unpaid,
As general cook and parlormaid

With seven funny little men,
Each one not more than three foot ten,
Ex-horse-race jockeys, all of them.
These Seven Dwarfs, though awfully nice,
Were guilty of one shocking vice—
They squandered all of their resources
At the race track backing horses.
(When they hadn't backed a winner,
None of them got any dinner.)
One evening, Snow White said, "Look here,
I think I've got a great idea.
Just leave it all to me, okay?
And no more gambling till I say."
That very night, at eventide,
Young Snow White hitched another ride,
And then, when it was very late,
She slipped in through the Palace gate.
The King was in the counting house
Counting out the money,
The Queen was in the parlor
Eating bread and honey,
The footmen and the servants slept
So no one saw her as she crept
On tip toe through the mighty hall
And grabbed THE MIRROR off the wall.
As soon as she had got it home,
She told the Senior Dwarf (or Gnome)
To ask it what he wished to know.
"Go on!" she shouted. "Have a go!"
He said, "Oh Mirror, please don't joke!
Each one of us is stony broke!
Which horse will win tomorrow's race,
The Ascot Gold Cup Steeplechase?"
The Mirror whispered sweet and low,
"The horse's name is Mistletoe."
The Dwarfs went absolutely daft,
They kissed young Snow White fore and aft,
Then rushed away to raise some dough
With which to back old Mistletoe.

They pawned their watches, sold the car,
They borrowed money near and far,
(For much of it they had to thank
The manager of Barclays Bank).
They went to Ascot and of course
For once they backed the winning horse.
Thereafter, every single day,
The Mirror made the bookies pay.
Each Dwarf and Snow White got a share,
And each was soon a millionaire,
Which shows that gambling's not a sin
Provided that you always win.

X. RUMPELSTILTSKIN

SARA HENDERSON HAY

The Name

One of my names, and I have many others,
Is Rumpelstiltskin. Desperate people call
On me for aid, by one's or by another's
Particular approach. I hear them all.
Facing a hopeless task, they cry to me.
I help them if I wish, or as I choose.
I'm sometimes swayed by whim, or flattery,
Or repetition of a phrase they use.

What touches me is that they so believe
A name invoked could have some magic power
To turn the clumsy spindle that they hold
Into a tool to avert the impending hour,
And give *me* credit, when their eyes perceive
What daily chaff and straw they've spun to gold!

ANNE SEXTON

Rumpelstiltskin

Inside many of us
is a small old man
who wants to get out.
No bigger than a two-year-old
whom you'd call lamb chop
yet this one is old and malformed.
His head is okay
but the rest of him wasn't Sanforized.
He is a monster of despair.
He is all decay.
He speaks up as tiny as an earphone
with Truman's asexual voice:
I am your dwarf.
I am the enemy within.
I am the boss of your dreams.
No. I am not the law in your mind,
the grandfather of watchfulness.
I am the law of your members,
the kindred of blackness and impulse.
See. Your hand shakes.
It is not palsy or booze.
It is your Doppelgänger
trying to get out.
Beware . . . Beware . . .

There once was a miller
with a daughter as lovely as a grape.
He told the king that she could
spin gold out of common straw.
The king summoned the girl
and locked her in a room full of straw
and told her to spin it into gold
or she would die like a criminal.
Poor grape with no one to pick.
Luscious and round and sleek.
Poor thing.
To die and never see Brooklyn.

She wept,
of course, huge aquamarine tears.
The door opened and in popped a dwarf.
He was as ugly as a wart.
Little thing, what are you? she cried.
With his tiny no-sex voice he replied:
I am a dwarf.
I have been exhibited on Bond Street
and no child will ever call me Papa.
I have no private life.
If I'm in my cups
the whole town knows by breakfast
and no child will ever call me Papa.
I am eighteen inches high.
I am no bigger than a partridge.
I am your evil eye
and no child will ever call me Papa.
Stop this Papa foolishness,
she cried. Can you perhaps
spin straw into gold?
Yes indeed, he said,
that I can do.
He spun the straw into gold
and she gave him her necklace
as a small reward.
When the king saw what she had done
he put her in a bigger room of straw
and threatened death once more.
Again she cried.
Again the dwarf came.
Again he spun the straw into gold.
She gave him her ring
as a small reward.
The king put her in an even bigger room
but this time he promised
to marry her if she succeeded.
Again she cried.

Again the dwarf came.
But she had nothing to give him.
Without a reward the dwarf would not spin.
He was on the scent of something bigger.
He was a regular bird dog.
Give me your first-born
and I will spin.
She thought: Piffle!
He is a silly little man.
And so she agreed.
So he did the trick.
Gold as good as Fort Knox.

The king married her
and within a year
a son was born.
He was like most new babies,
as ugly as an artichoke
but the queen thought him a pearl.
She gave him her dumb lactation,
delicate, trembling, hidden,
warm, etc.
And then the dwarf appeared
to claim his prize.
Indeed! I have become a papa!
cried the little man.
She offered him all the kingdom
but he wanted only this—
a living thing
to call his own.
And being mortal
who can blame him?

The queen cried two pails of sea water.
She was as persistent
as a Jehovah's Witness.
And the dwarf took pity.

He said: I will give you
three days to guess my name
and if you cannot do it
I will collect your child.
The queen sent messengers
throughout the land to find
names of the most unusual sort.
When he appeared the next day
she asked: Melchior?
Balthazar?
But each time the dwarf replied:
No! No! That's not my name.
The next day she asked:
Spindleshanks? Spiderlegs?
But it was still no-no.
On the third day the messenger
came back with a strange story.
He told her:
As I came around the corner of the wood
where the fox says good night to the hare
I saw a little house with a fire
burning in front of it.
Around that fire a ridiculous little man
was leaping on one leg and singing:
Today I bake.
Tomorrow I brew my beer.
The next day the queen's only child will be mine.
Not even the census taker knows
that Rumpelstiltskin is my name . . .
The queen was delighted.
She had the name!
Her breath blew bubbles.

When the dwarf returned
she called out:
Is your name by any chance Rumpelstiltskin?
He cried: The devil told you that!

He stamped his right foot into the ground
and sank in up to his waist.
Then he tore himself in two.
Somewhat like a split broiler.
He laid his two sides down on the floor,
one part soft as a woman,
one part a barbed hook,
one part papa,
one part Doppelgänger.

WILLIAM HATHAWAY

Rumplestiltskin Poems

In Dead Air, Under Furious Sun

In dead air, under furious sun
we play ball soaked in ourselves.
This is the angry game of gutterals
when we beg viscera, cajole muscle
to at once make us beautiful again.

The crummy bums stumble, eyes
like mouth go milky; mucous-makers.
But no crybabies, everything's wet
in that south except those furnace eyes,
snake dry; sizzling spit in the dust.

Once I danced in a field pounding aim-
less declensions in a glove and sang
snatches of tunes of terror and glory.
No hideous chasm opened when I stamped
defeat and like a thick roar the air took me.

We always forgive the body and curse the spirit,
but in reptilian pride condescend to both.
I taste bitter guts after every run. Only
courage can pace out tedious lines for fun.
Like this dwarf whose legs are not enough

to carry him where balls laze to the earth,
and everywhere he runs is a bloated laugh.
Never forgive! The atoms themselves are untouchable
and I demand the princess in the stands. Or else
my awful stamp will bury all names still unsung.

Rumplestiltskin's Plan

So lonely he'd kiss maggots from the mouth
of a dead trick, weeping in disgust and passion.
On a chair he moons the sink mirror, straining
for a second of romance. Not so warped but
curious, and if they isolate the soul like
mind and body it couldn't be lonelier; more airy.

When a reporter-at-large asked about mini-skirts
Rumplestiltskin said "Va-Va-Va-Voom!" but his
heart wasn't in it. His sad eyes counted sidewalk
squares, parking meters, everything but bobbing
asses that crammed, overflowed all his opinions.
When salesgirls smile linoleum pukes aisles away.

Guts in his teeth he opens "You don't know me
but my name is ________." Fault in the line because
this game is serious, the sacred name of a game.
As a peeper he hears a peepee say "Love lies
in my clitoris dear" and "Awright I love your
clitoris then." When springs jangle Rumplestiltskin

cries tears pink with blood, gnashes yellows
and perfects his scheme. He'll buy beauty young,
raise her dumb, and fuck stars in her lovely eyes.
For him there are but a few sweet seconds in all
this life. Past and future are one blank chasm,
so in seconds is his final, secret name.

The Gold Factory

"You're a hell of a temple" he said,
shaving around the warts. Inside
a flash of longing like electricity
arcing through a vacuum bell.
Later in the Volks (What else would
he drive?) bitter words for sunlight,
stomping raised pedals with furious feet.
"Eat some screw" to the old gateman;
"You smell like B.O." to the teenage
office girl. After lunch the old sardine
can goes in the toilet; he takes a dump.
But from all over California they cart straw,
and huge machines spin out GOLD so pure
tires burst under folks chuckling to the bank.
Immodest in rage, not money or power
Rumplestiltskin eats one fried egg a night
with salt and ketchup in his humble hut.
Then the all-night squirm in his crib
under the snail-slimy moon he mutters
"My name, ho-ho. You'll never know *my* name!"

Liar Rumplestiltskin Loves

Folding chairs, a tennis bench
for table and wine chilled
in the little stream set the scene.
I forgot stars, stars and a yellow moon.
Moon blazing off her tennis dress
that he ached to lift with anemone
fingers until she sang like a wolf.
She thinks his name is Jewish, respects
him too much for funny biz quite yet.
Jesus! How flesh dances perfectly
in tune with swell and thump of blood.
Those small breasts poking when she's back
for the serve, hard rump pistoning
on the charge to the net; to him.
In thin air and thudding ears insects sing.
Nobody understands—days of parents,
friends, professionals, who live to take.
Because he is a swart man and only handsome
in gaps between his teeth the cold
hand should breeze into his moist palm.
He could fall pissing into that stream,
go clean as waterbabies, Little English
Boy. Rumplestiltskin never does that.
A tennis ball keeps him afloat
while he threads between dark shapes
into the pipe of cobwebs, stinking
of tar where light at the end seems
brilliant as day and rocks are so ready
for the stamping of little feet.

Antistrophe

Dishonest men are always the rage
in glorious and exultant ambush.
They say "fat, fat, I am the personal"
pointing to hens, foxes, storks
with winking wisdom of fabulists.
"Screw you guys" said Rumplestiltskin
and he stomped off into the sunset.

Always a man to take a myth seriously,
he fingered the mossy trees. Seemed real.
Back where a giant hand stamped five lakes
in the forest he'd learned a little toad, too.
They speak when squeezed. Never squeeze.
It seemed his disloyal friend was casting
into an icy cirque and cursing luck.

There are moments of trinity in our lives,
when the body and spirit discuss the present
while we sit and fidget like uneducated guests.
Rumplestiltskin prefers to tumble perpetually
into that black moment in love and singing.
Days and nights whirl by to that first kiss
so full of promise and surprise.

XI. SNOW WHITE AND ROSE RED

DENISE LEVERTOV

An Embroidery

Rose Red's hair is brown as fur
and shines in firelight as she prepares
supper of honey and apples, curds and whey,
for the bear, and leaves it ready
on the hearth-stone.

Rose White's grey eyes
look into the dark forest.

Rose Red's cheeks are burning,
sign of her ardent, joyful
compassionate heart.
Rose White is pale,
turning away when she hears
the bear's paw on the latch.

When he enters, there is
frost on his fur,
he draws near to the fire
giving off sparks.
Rose White catches the scent of the forest,
of mushrooms, of rosin.

Together Rose Red and Rose White
sing to the bear;
it is a cradle song, a loom song,
a song about marriage, about
a pilgrimage to the mountains
long ago.
                Raised on an elbow,
the bear stretched on the hearth
nods and hums; soon he sighs
and puts down his head.

He sleeps; the Roses
bank the fire.
Sunk in the clouds of their feather bed
they prepare to dream.

Rose Red in a cave that smells of honey
dreams she is combing the fur of her cubs
with a golden comb.
Rose White is lying awake.

Rose White shall marry the bear's brother.
Shall he too
when the time is ripe,
step from the bear's hide?
Is that other, her bridegroom,
here in the room?

BARBARA UNGER

Breasts

sisters
Snow White and Rose Red
you are the two
sides of the coin
mother tossed up
for luck
landing
heads first.

held up
between the fingers
they are erect
flesh to contend.
two soldiers,
twat-assed
in miniskirts.

or else for
ladypoets to stuff
soggy tissues
between, tear-stained.

pillows to stroke.
Dugs to be
sucked.
jellyfish to spawn.

Tugging us back
again and again
Into our own mothers,
Beginning, drying, dying.

Mouths that clutch arms
And some primal mother
that encircles us all
Like a tree that fissures
Out of the center of all things.

JOAN COLBY

Rose Red to Snow White

A dark wind batters the door,
our minds unchink as
the chimney roars and the eaves
shriek in their rusty dreams.

Huddle by the fire, sister,
something is snapping in the applewood
and sparks ignite our nightgowns.
Let us save each other.
Let us marry these ashes.

Don't leave the comfort we've found
for that rap on the doorjamb.
God knows who'd be out
on such a night, in a blizzard
like this one. Have no pity
on travelers far from town
in this fierce weather.

But you've unlatched us,
let a whirlwind of white flakes
confuse our destinies
and succored a brute of fur
whose snout embeds
in your fabulous hair.

A thorn stabs
my red heart
as you lie down
with the great bear
bringing him to life
with your white body.

How can you be sure
he'll turn at last into something
noble, that he won't always
raid your breasts for honey
or sleep grunting all winter.

REFERENCES:
Biographical and Bibliographical

I include here publication information for the poems and where possible their dates as well as the dates of the respective authors. For some of the more obscure poets these dates were not available.

Abse, Dannie (born 1923)
"Pantomime Diseases" (1979).
Poetry 133, no. 5 (1979), p. 264.

Ahmed-ud-Din, Feroz (born 1949)
"Cinderella" (1974).
This Handful of Dust. Calcutta, India: Writers Workshop, 1974, p. 16.

Brewster, Elizabeth (born 1922)
"The Princess Addresses The Frog Prince."
Mountain Moving Day: Poems by Women. Edited by Elaine Gill. Trumansburg, N.Y.: Crossing Press, 1973, p. 36.

Broumas, Olga (born 1949)
"Cinderella," "Rapunzel," "Little Red Riding Hood," "Snow White" (1977).
Beginning with O. New Haven: Yale University Press, 1977, pp. 57–58, 59–60, 67–68, 69–71.

Carruth, Hayden (born 1921)
"Dornröschen (The Sleeping Beauty)" (1982).
The Sleeping Beauty. New York: Harper and Row, 1982, p. 48.

Carryl, Guy Wetmore (1873–1904)
"Red Riding Hood."
The Home Book of Verse. Edited by Burton E. Stevenson. New York: Holt, Rinehart and Winston, 1953, pp. 2077–79.

Caskey, Noelle
"Ripening" (1979).
Berkeley Poets Cooperative 16 (1979), p. 20.

Chasin, Helen
"Mythics."
I Hear My Sisters Saying. Edited by Carol Konek and Dorothy Walters. New York: Thomas Y. Crowell, 1976, pp. 174–77.

Chute, Robert M. (born 1926)
"Snow White" (1967).
Quest 2, no. 2 (1967), p. 148.

Cohen, Leonard (born 1934)
"The Sleeping Beauty" (1961).
Canadian Anthology. Edited by Carl E. Klinck and Reginald E. Watters. Toronto: W. J. Gage, 1966, p. 486.

Colby, Joan
"Rose Red to Snow White" (1976).
Wisconsin Review 11, no. 2 (1976), p. 19.

Corn, Alfred (born 1943)
"Dreambooks" (1974).
Poetry 123, no. 4 (1974), pp. 209–11.

Dahl, Roald (born 1916)
"Snow White and the Seven Dwarfs," "Little Red Riding Hood and the Wolf" (1982).
Revolting Rhymes. New York: Alfred A. Knopf, 1983, pp. 11–17, 30–34.

Davidman, Joy
"The Princess in the Ivory Tower" (1938).
Letter to a Comrade. New Haven: Yale University Press, 1938, p. 24.

Dickey, William (born 1928)
"The Dolls Play at Hansel and Gretel" (1959).
Of the Festivity. New York: AMS Press, 1971, pp. 3–7.

Ditsky, John (born 1938)
"Epithalamium" (1979).
Poem, no. 37 (1979), p. 46.

Farjeon, Eleanor (1881–1965)
"Coach."
A Pocketful of Rhymes. Edited by Katherine Love. New York: Thomas Y. Crowell, 1946, pp. 54–55.

Fisher, Aileen (born 1906)
"Cinderella Grass" (1980).
Put in the Dark and Daylight. New York: Harper and Row, 1980, p. 114.

Flanders, Jane (born 1940)
"Fairy Tales" (1978).
The Literary Review 21, no. 3 (1978), p. 338.

Ford, Sara de
"The Sleeping Beauty" (1969).
Poetry 114, no. 3 (1969), p. 171.

Freeman, Arthur (born 1938)
"Beauty, Sleeping" (1962).
Poetry 100, no. 5 (1962), pp. 293–94.

French, Mary Blake
"Ella of the Cinders."
Convocation! Women in Writing. Edited by Valerie Harms. Tampa: United Sisters, 1975, p. 98.

Gillespie, Robert (born 1938)

"Snow White" (1971).

New Voices in American Poetry: An Anthology. Edited by David Allan Evans. Cambridge, Mass.: Winthrop Publishers, 1973, pp. 94–96.

Glück, Louise (born 1943)

"Gretel in Darkness" (1971).

The House on Marshland. New York: Ecco Press, 1971, p. 5.

Graves, Robert (born 1895)

"The Frog and the Golden Ball" (c. 1964).

Collected Poems 1975. London: Cassell and Co., 1975, p. 420.

Hall, Donald (born 1928)

"Mirror" (1956).

New Poems by American Poets, vol. 2. Edited by Rolfe Humphries. Freeport, N.Y.: Books for Libraries Press, 1957, p. 66.

Hathaway, William (born 1944)

"Rumplestiltskin Poems" (1975).

A Wilderness of Monkeys. Ithaca, N.Y.: Ithaca House, 1975, pp. 42–46.

Hay, Sara Henderson (born 1906)

"The Sleeper," "The Marriage," "The Name," "Rapunzel," "One of the Seven Has Somewhat to Say," "Juvenile Court," "Interview," "The Princess," "The Benefactors" (1963).

Story Hour. Fayetteville: University of Arkansas Press, 1982, pp. 6–7, 11, 14, 18, 20, 26, 32, 38, 40.

Hill, Hyacinthe

"Rebels from Fairy Tales."

The Writing on the Wall. Edited by Walter Lowenfels. Garden City, N.Y.: Doubleday, 1969, p. 74.

Hillyer, Robert S. (1895–1961)

"And When the Prince Came."

The Collected Verse of Robert S. Hillyer. New York: Alfred A. Knopf, 1934, pp. 27–28.

Hope, A. D. (born 1907)

"Coup de Grâce."

Poetry, Past and Present. Edited by Frank Brady and Martin Price. New York: Harcourt, Brace, Jovanovich, 1974, pp. 381–82.

Hussey, Anne

"Cinderella" (1974).

Best Poems of 1974. Edited by Waddell Austin et al. Palo Alto, Calif.: Pacific Books, 1975, p. 71.

Hutton, Mary

"The Sleeping Beauty" (1951).

Poctry 78, no. 2 (1951), pp. 84–85.

Jarrell, Randall (1914–65)
"The Märchen (Grimm's Tales)" (c. 1945), "The Sleeping Beauty: Variation of the Prince" (1948), "Cinderella" (1960).
The Complete Poems. New York: Farrar, Straus and Giroux, 1969, pp. 82–85, 95–96, 217–18.

Johnson, Charles (born 1948)
"Sleeping Beauty" (1969).
I Heard a Scream in the Street: Poems of Young People in the City. Edited by Nancy Larrick. New York: M. Evans, 1970, p. 104.

Jones, Paul R. (born 1946)
"Becoming a Frog" (1975).
The End of the Hand. Washington, D.C.: Word Works, 1975, p. 19.

Kallman, Chester Simon (1921–75)
"Tellers of Tales" (1957).
Absent and Present. Middletown, Conn.: Wesleyan University Press, 1957, p. 67.

Kinnell, Galway (born 1927)
"Kissing the Toad" (1980).
Mortal Acts, Mortal Words. Boston: Houghton Mifflin, 1980, p. 25.

Knight, Douglas (born 1921)
"Sleeping Beauty: August" (1968).
Texas Quarterly 11, no. 3 (1968), p. 206.

Kumin, Maxine (born 1925)
"The Archaeology of a Marriage" (1978).
Poetry 132, no. 1 (1978), pp. 3–4.

La Mare, Walter de (1873–1956)
"Sleeping Beauty" (1901).
Collected Poems 1901–1918, vol. 2. New York: Henry Holt, 1920, p. 72.

Levertov, Denise (born 1923)
"An Embroidery."
Partisan Review 34, no. 4 (1967), pp. 547–48.

Locklin, Gerald (born 1941)
"The Dwarf" (1966).
Western Humanities Review 20, no. 3 (1966), p. 220.

Mandel, Eli (born 1922)
"Rapunzel (Girl in a Tower)."
Black and Secret Man. Toronto: Ryerson Press, 1964, p. 29.

Mayo, E. L. (born 1904)
"The Sleeping Beauty" (1958).
Summer Unbound and Other Poems. Minneapolis: University of Minnesota Press, 1958, p. 20.

Meyer, Gerard Previn (born 1909)
"Rapunzel Song."
The New York Times Book of Verse. Edited by Thomas Lask. New York: Macmillan, 1970, p. 93.

Miller, John N. (born 1933)
"Prince Charming" (1969).
Poetry 114, no. 6 (1969), p. 379.

Mitchell, Roger (born 1935)
"Cinderella" (1980).
Poetry 137, no. 3 (1980), pp. 149–50.

Mitchell, Susan
"From the Journals of the Frog Prince" (1978).
New Yorker (May 15, 1978), p. 40.

Morgan, Robin (born 1941)
"The Two Gretels" (1976).
Lady of the Beasts. New York: Random House, 1976, p. 51.

Mueller, Lisel (born 1924)
"Reading the Brothers Grimm to Jenny" (c. 1976).
The Private Life. Baton Rouge: Louisiana State University Press, 1976, pp. 5–6.

Nemerov, Howard (born 1920)
"Sleeping Beauty."
New and Selected Poems. Chicago: University of Chicago Press, 1973, p. 39.

O'Conor, Norreys Jephson (1885–1958)
"To a Child (With a Copy of the Author's 'Hansel and Gretel')."
The Home Book of Modern Verse. Edited by Burton E. Stevenson. New York: Henry Holt, 1926, pp. 37–38.

Owen, Wilfred (1893–1918)
"The Sleeping Beauty" (1914).
The Collected Poems of Wilfred Owen. Edited by C. Day Lewis. London: Chatto and Windus, 1963, p. 132.

Ower, John (born 1942)
"The Gingerbread House" (1979).
Kansas Quarterly 11, nos. 1–2 (1979), p. 70.

Pack, Robert (born 1929)
"The Frog Prince (A Speculation on Grimm's Fairy Tale)." (1980).
Waking to My Name. New and Selected Poems. Baltimore: Johns Hopkins University Press, 1980, p. 246.

Pettingell, Phoebe
"Frog Prince" (1972).
Poetry 120, no. 3 (1972), p. 138.

Pickard, Cynthia
"Cinderella."
Poetry for Pleasure. The Hallmark Book of Poetry. Selected and arranged by the editors of Hallmark Cards, Inc. Garden City, N.Y.: Doubleday, 1960, p. 59.
Plath, Sylvia (1932–1963)
"Cinderella."
The Collected Poems. Sylvia Plath. Edited by Ted Hughes. New York: Harper and Row, 1981, pp. 303–4.
Ray, David (born 1932)
"Hansel and Gretel Return" (c. 1966).
Dragging the Main and Other Poems. Ithaca, N.Y.: Cornell University Press, 1968, p. 43.
Reid, Dorothy E. (born 1900)
"Coach into Pumpkin" (1925).
Coach into Pumpkin. New York: AMS Press, 1971, p. 40.
Richardson, Dorothy Lee (born 1900)
"Modern Grimm" (1949).
Poetry 73, no. 5 (1949), pp. 275–76.
Riley, James Whitcomb (1849–1916)
"A Sleeping Beauty," "Maymie's Story of Red Riding Hood."
The Complete Works of James Whitcomb Riley, vols. 2, 7. New York: Harper, 1916, 2: 464–65; 7: 1768–74.
Roberts, Elizabeth Madox (1881–1941)
"Cinderella's Song."
A Pocketful of Rhymes. Edited by Katherine Love. New York: Thomas Y. Crowell, 1946, p. 54.
Sexton, Anne (1928–74)
"Snow White and the Seven Dwarfs" (c. 1970), "Rumpelstiltskin" (1971), "Rapunzel" (1971), "Little Red Riding Hood" (1971), "The Frog Prince" (1971).
Transformations. Boston: Houghton Mifflin, 1971, pp. 3–9, 17–22, 35–42, 73–79, 93–99.
Sheck, Laurie
"Sleeping Beauty" (1979).
Poetry Northwest 20, no. 1 (1979), pp. 38–39.
Shore, Jane (born 1947)
"Sleeping Beauty" (1981).
Poetry 137, no. 6 (1981), pp. 324–25.
Sklarew, Myra (born 1934)
"Red Riding Hood at the Acropolis" (1973).
Carolina Quarterly 25, no. 3 (1973), pp. 42–43.
Smith, Stevie (1902–71)
"The Frog Prince" (1966).
The Best Beast. New York: Alfred A. Knopf, 1969, pp. 14–16.

Swift, Joan (born 1926)
"Vancouver Island" (1966).
Literary Review 10, no. 1 (1966), pp. 81–82.

Thompson, Phyllis (born 1926)
"A Fairy Tale" (1969).
Artichoke and Other Poems. Honolulu: University of Hawaii Press, 1969, p. 8.

Unger, Barbara (born 1932)
"Breasts" (1973).
Wisconsin Review 9, no. 3 (1973), p. 10.

Untermeyer, Louis (1885–1977)
"Rapunzel."
The New Adam. New York: Harcourt, Brace and Howe, 1920, p. 57.

Watson, Evelyn M. (1886–1954)
"A Sleeping Beauty" (1931).
Symbols of Immortality. Boston: Christopher Publishing House, 1931, p. 50.

Weaver, Edith
"Lost Cinderella" (1947).
Poetry 70, no. 2 (1947), pp. 69–70.

White, Gail (born 1945)
"Happy Endings" (1978).
Poem, no. 34 (November 1978), p. 10.

Wylie, Elinor (1885–1928)
"Sleeping Beauty."
Collected Poems of Elinor Wylie. New York: Alfred A. Knopf, 1947, p. 246.

Zupan, Vitomil (born 1914)
"A Fairy Tale" (1971).
Literary Review 14, no. 3 (1971), p. 298.

ACKNOWLEDGMENTS

Considerable effort was made to locate the holders of copyright for the poems in this book. For the most part we were successful and have acknowledged below their permissions to reprint these works. However, in a few instances we were unable to trace the copyright holders. In such cases we have listed the periodical or book from which we reprinted these poems. We welcome information that would help us trace these copyright holders and regret that we could not include our thanks to them.

Also, a number of poems which might have been in this volume could not be included due to the difficulty of negotiating permissions to reprint them from the copyright holders.

Dannie Abse, p. 20. "Pantomime Diseases" by Dannie Abse from *One-Legged on Ice*, copyright © 1983 by Dannie Abse, published by University of Georgia Press. Used by permission of University of Georgia Press and the editor of *Poetry*. Originally published in *Poetry*, vol. 133, no. 5 (1979). **Feroz Ahmed-ud-Din**, p. 82. "Cinderella" by Feroz Ahmed-ud-Din is reprinted from *This Handful of Dust*, published by the Writers Workshop, Calcutta, India, in 1974. **Elizabeth Brewster**, p. 36. "The Princess Addresses the Frog Prince" by Elizabeth Brewster from *In Search of Eros* used by permission of Irwin Publishing Inc. Copyright © 1974 by Clarke, Irwin & Company Ltd. **Olga Broumas**, pp. 55, 85, 111, 160. "Rapunzel," "Cinderella," "Little Red Riding Hood," and "Snow White" by Olga Broumas from *Beginning with O* used with permission of Yale University Press. **Hayden Carruth**, p. 145. "Dornröschen (The Sleeping Beauty)" by Hayden Carruth from *The Sleeping Beauty* used by permission of Harper & Row, Publishers, Inc. Copyright © 1982 by Hayden Carruth. **Guy Wetmore Carryl**, p. 100. "Red Riding Hood" by Guy Wetmore Carryl is reprinted from *The Home Book of Verse*, published by Holt, Rinehart, and Winston in 1953, where it appeared by permission of Harper & Brothers. **Noelle Caskey**, p. 142. "Ripening" by Noelle Caskey from *Berkeley Poets Cooperative*, vol. 16 (1979) used by permission of Berkeley Poets Workshop and Press. **Helen Chasin**, p. 15. "Mythics" by

Helen Chasin is reprinted from *I Hear My Sisters Saying*, published by Thomas Y. Crowell Company in 1976. **Robert M. Chute**, p. 152. "Snow White" by Robert M. Chute from *The Quest*, vol. 2, no. 2 (1967) used by permission of the author. **Leonard Cohen**, p. 129. "The Sleeping Beauty" by Leonard Cohen from *The Spice Box of the Earth* used by permission of Viking Penguin, Inc. and The Canadian Publishers, McClelland and Stewart Ltd., Toronto. Copyright © 1961 by McClelland and Stewart. **Joan Colby**, p. 186. "Rose Red to Snow White" by Joan Colby is reprinted from *Wisconsin Review*, vol. 11, no. 2 (1976). **Alfred Corn**, p. 10. "Dreambooks" by Alfred Corn from *All Roads at Once*, Viking Press, 1976. Used by permission of the author. Copyright © Alfred Corn. **Roald Dahl**, pp. 113, 163. "Little Red Riding Hood" and "Snow White and the Seven Dwarfs" by Roald Dahl from *Revolting Rhymes*, illustrated by Quentin Blake, used by permission of Alfred A. Knopf, Inc. and Jonathan Cape Ltd. Copyright © 1982 by Roald Dahl. **Joy Davidman**, p. 46. "The Princess in the Ivory Tower" by Joy Davidman from *Letter to a Comrade* used by permission of Yale University Press. **Sara de Ford**, p. 135. "The Sleeping Beauty" by Sara de Ford from *Poetry*, vol. 114, no. 3 (1969) used by permission of the editor of *Poetry* and the author. Copyright © 1969 by the Modern Poetry Association. **Walter de la Mare**, p. 117. "Sleeping Beauty" by Walter de la Mare is reprinted from *Collected Poems 1901–1918*, published by Henry Holt in 1916. **William Dickey**, p. 61. "The Dolls Play at Hansel and Gretel" by William Dickey from *Of the Festivity* (Yale University Press, 1959) used by permission of the author. **John Ditsky**, p. 140. "Epithalamium" by John Ditsky is reprinted from *Poem*, no. 37 (1979). **Eleanor Farjeon**, p. 75. "Coach" by Eleanor Farjeon is reprinted from *A Pocketful of Rhymes*, published by Thomas Y. Crowell Company in 1946. **Aileen Fisher**, p. 91. "Cinderella Grass" by Aileen Fisher from *Out in the Dark and Daylight* used by permission of Harper & Row, Publishers, Inc. Copyright © 1980 by Aileen Fisher. **Jane Flanders**, p. 18. "Fairy Tales" by Jane Flanders from *The Literary Review*, vol. 21, no. 3 (1978), published by Fairleigh Dickinson University, used by permission of *The Literary Review* and the author. **Arthur**

Freeman, p. 130. "Beauty, Sleeping" by Arthur Freeman is reprinted from *Poetry*, vol. 100, no. 5 (1962). **Mary Blake French**, p. 84. "Ella of the Cinders" by Mary Blake French from *Convocation! Women in Writing*, United Sisters Press, used by permission of the author. **Robert Gillespie**, p. 153. "Snow White" by Robert Gillespie from *Wisconsin Review*, vol. 6, no. 2 (1971) used by permission of *Wisconsin Review*. **Louise Glück**, p. 68. "Gretel in Darkness" by Louise Glück from *The House of Marshland* used by permission of The Ecco Press. Copyright © 1975 by Louise Glück. **Robert Graves**, p. 24. "The Frog and the Golden Ball" by Robert Graves from *Collected Poems 1975* used by permission of A. P. Watt Ltd., Literary Agents. **Donald Hall**, p. 149. "Mirror" by Donald Hall used by permission of the author. Copyright © 1957 by Donald Hall. **William Hathaway**, p. 175. "Rumplestiltskin Poems" by William Hathaway from *A Wilderness of Monkeys* used by permission of Ithaca House. Copyright © 1975 by Ithaca House. **Sara Henderson Hay**, pp. 2, 3, 23, 47, 66, 81, 131, 150, 169. "The Benefactors," "The Princess," "The Marriage," "Rapunzel," "Juvenile Court," "Interview," "The Sleeper," "One of the Seven Has Somewhat to Say," and "The Name" by Sara Henderson Hay are reprinted from *Story Hour*, copyright © 1982 by Sara Henderson Hay. Used by permission of Universisty of Arkansas Press. **Hyacinthe Hill**, p. 27. "Rebels from Fairy Tales" by Hyacinthe Hill from *The Writing on the Wall*, edited by Walter Lowenfels, published by Doubleday in 1969, used by permission of Manna Lowenfels, literary executrix for the Estate of Walter Lowenfels. **Robert S. Hillyer**, p. 124. "And When the Prince Came" by Robert S. Hillyer from *The Collected Verse of Robert S. Hillyer* used by permission of Alfred A. Knopf, Inc. Copyright © 1933, renewed 1961, by Robert S. Hillyer. **A. D. Hope**, p. 102. "Coup de Grâce" by A. D. Hope from *A. D. Hope Collected Poems* is reprinted with permission of Angus & Robertson (UK) Ltd. **Anne Hussey**, p. 83. "Cinderella" by Anne Hussey is reprinted from *Baddeck and Other Poems*, published by Wesleyan University Press, 1978. It originally appeared in *The New Yorker* (August 19, 1974). **Mary Hutton**, p. 127. "The Sleeping Beauty" by Mary Hutton is reprinted from *Poetry*, vol. 78, no. 2 (1951).

Randall Jarrell, pp. 6, 77, 125. "The Märchen (Grimm's Tales)" and "The Sleeping Beauty: Variation of the Prince" from *The Complete Poems* by Randall Jarrell. Copyright © 1946, 1948 by Mrs. Randall Jarrell. Copyright renewed 1974, 1975 by Mrs. Randall Jarrell. Reprinted by permission of Farrar, Straus & Giroux, Inc. and Faber and Faber Ltd. Randall Jarrell, "Cinderella" from *The Woman at the Washington Zoo*. Copyright © 1960 Randall Jarrell. Reprinted with the permission of Atheneum publishers. "Cinderella" reprinted by permission of Faber and Faber Ltd. from *The Complete Poems* by Randall Jarrell. **Charles Johnson**, p. 136. "Sleeping Beauty" by Charles Johnson is reprinted from *I Heard a Scream in the Street: Poems of Young People in the City*, edited by Nancy Larrick, published in 1970 by M. Evans and Company, Inc. **Paul R. Jones**, p. 37. "Becoming a Frog" by Paul R. Jones is reprinted from *The End of the Hand*, published in 1975 by The Word Works. **Chester Simon Kallman**, p. 1. "Tellers of Tales" by Chester Simon Kallman reprinted from *Absent and Present* by permission of Wesleyan University Press. Copyright © 1963 by Chester Simon Kallman. **Galway Kinnell**, p. 41. "Kissing the Toad" by Galway Kinnell from *Mortal Acts, Mortal Words* used by permission of Houghton Mifflin Company. Copyright © 1980 by Galway Kinnell. **Douglas Knight**, p. 134. "Sleeping Beauty: August" by Douglas Knight from *The Texas Quarterly*, vol. 11, no. 3 (1968) used by permission of University of Texas Press and the author. **Maxine Kumin**, p. 138. "Archaeology of a Marriage" by Maxine Kumin from *The Retrieval System* used by permission of Viking Penguin, Inc. Copyright © 1978 by Maxine Kumin. **Denise Levertov**, p. 183. "An Embroidery" by Denise Levertov first appeared in *Partisan Review*, vol. 34, no. 4 (1967), pages 547–48. Used with permission of *Partisan Review*. **Gerald Locklin**, p. 151. "The Dwarf" by Gerald Locklin from *Western Humanities Review*, vol. 20, no. 3 (1966) used by permission of *Western Humanities Review*. **Eli Mandel**, p. 48. "Rapunzel (Girl in a Tower)" by Eli Mandel from *Black and Secret Man* used by permission of McGraw-Hill Ryerson Ltd. **E. L. Mayo**, p. 128. "The Sleeping Beauty" by E. L. Mayo from *Summer Unbound and Other Poems* used by permission of University of

Minnesota Press. **Gerard Previn Meyer**, p. 49. "Rapunzel Song" by Gerard Previn Meyer from *The New York Times Book of Verse*, published by Macmillan Publishing Company in 1970, used by permission of the author. **John N. Miller**, p. 29. "Prince Charming" by John N. Miller from *Poetry*, vol. 114, no. 6 (1969) used by permission of the editor of *Poetry* and the author. Copyright © 1969 by the Modern Poetry Association. **Roger Mitchell**, p. 87. "Cinderella" by Roger Mitchell from *Poetry*, vol. 137, no. 3 (1980) used by permission of the editor of *Poetry* and the author. Copyright © 1980 by the Modern Poetry Association. **Susan Mitchell**, p. 38. "From the Journals of the Frog Prince" by Susan Mitchell from *The Water Inside the Water* (Wesleyan University Press, 1983), originally in *The New Yorker* (May 15, 1978). Used by permission of *The New Yorker*. Copyright © 1978 by Susan Mitchell. **Robin Morgan**, p. 69. "The Two Gretels" by Robin Morgan from *Lady of the Beasts* used by permission of Random House, Inc. and the author c/o Edite Kroll. Copyright © 1976 by Robin Morgan. **Lisel Mueller**, p. 4. "Reading the Brothers Grimm to Jenny" by Lisel Mueller from *The Private Life* (Louisiana State University Press, 1976), first published in *The New Yorker*. Used by permission of Louisiana State University Press. Copyright © 1967 by Lisel Mueller. **Howard Nemerov**, p. 137. "Sleeping Beauty" by Howard Nemerov from *The Collected Poems of Howard Nemerov* (University of Chicago Press, 1977) used by permission of the author. **Norreys Jephson O'Conor**, p. 59. "To a Child (With a Copy of the Author's 'Hansel and Gretel')" by Norreys Jephson O'Conor reprinted from *The Home Book of Modern Verse*, published by Henry Holt in 1926. **Wilfred Owen**, p. 118. "The Sleeping Beauty" by Wilfred Owen reprinted from *The Collected Poems of Wilfred Owen*, published by Chatto and Windus in 1963. **John Ower**, p. 70. "The Gingerbread House" by John Ower from *Kansas Quarterly*, vol. 11, nos. 1–2 (1979) by permission of *Kansas Quarterly*. **Robert Pack**, p. 40. "The Frog Prince (A Speculation on Grimm's Fairy Tale)" by Robert Pack from *Waking to My Name: New and Selected Poems*, used by permission of The Johns Hopkins University Press. Copyright © 1980 by The Johns Hopkins University Press.

Phoebe Pettingell, p. 35. "Frog Prince" by Phoebe Pettingell from *Poetry*, vol. 120, no. 3 (1972) used by permission of the editor of *Poetry* and the author. Copyright © 1972 by the Modern Poetry Association. **Cynthia Pickard**, p. 79. "Cinderella" by Cynthia Pickard is reprinted from *Poetry for Pleasure: The Hallmark Book of Poetry*, published by Doubleday in 1960. **Sylvia Plath**, p. 80. "Cinderella" by Sylvia Plath from *The Collected Poems of Sylvia Plath*, edited by Ted Hughes, used by permission of Harper & Row, Publishers, Inc. and Olwyn Hughes Literary Agency. Copyright © 1981 by Ted Hughes. **David Ray**, p. 67. "Hansel and Gretel Return" by David Ray from *Dragging the Main and Other Poems*, Cornell University Press, used by permission of the author. Copyright © 1984 by David Ray. **Dorothy E. Reid**, p. 73. "Coach into Pumpkin" by Dorothy E. Reid is reprinted from *Coach into Pumpkin*, published by AMS Press in 1971. **Dorothy Lee Richardson**, p. 60. "Modern Grimm" by Dorothy Lee Richardson from *Poetry*, vol. 73, no. 5 (1949) used by permission of the editor of *Poetry* and the author. Copyright © 1949 by the Modern Poetry Association. **James Whitcomb Riley**, pp. 95, 119. "Maymie's Story of Red Riding Hood" and "A Sleeping Beauty" by James Whitcomb Riley reprinted from *The Collected Works of James Whitcomb Riley*, published by Harper in 1916. **Elizabeth Madox Roberts**, p. 74. "Cinderella's Song" by Elizabeth Madox Roberts is reprinted from *A Pocketful of Rhymes*, published by Thomas Y. Crowell Company in 1946. **Anne Sexton**, pp. 30, 50, 103, 155, 170. "The Frog Prince," "Rapunzel," "Little Red Riding Hood," "Snow White and the Seven Dwarfs," and "Rumpelstiltskin" are from *Transformations* by Anne Sexton. Copyright © 1971 by Anne Sexton. Reprinted by permission of the Houghton Mifflin Company and the Sterling Lord Agency, Inc. **Laurie Sheck**, p. 141. "Sleeping Beauty" by Laurie Sheck from *Amaranth*, copyright © 1981 by University of Georgia Press, used by permission of University of Georgia Press. **Jane Shore**, p. 143. "Sleeping Beauty" by Jane Shore from *Poetry*, vol. 137, no. 6 (1981) used by permission of the editor of *Poetry* and the author. Copyright © 1981 by the Modern Poetry Association. **Myra Sklarew**, p. 109. "Red Riding Hood at the Acropolis" by Myra Sklarew from *Carolina Quarterly*, vol. 25, no. 3 (1973) used by permission of *Carolina Quarterly*. **Stevie Smith**, p. 25. "The Frog Prince" by Stevie Smith from *Collected Poems* used by permission of New Directions Publishing Corp. and James MacGibbon, executor of the Stevie Smith Estate. Copyright © 1972 by Stevie Smith. **Joan Swift**, p. 133. "Vancouver Island" by Joan Swift from *The Literary Review*, vol. 10, no. 1 (1966), published by Fairleigh Dickinson University, used by permission of *The Literary Review* and the author. Copyright by Joan Swift. **Phyllis Thompson**, p. 28. "A Fairy Tale" by Phyllis Thompson from *Artichoke and Other Poems* used by permission of the University of Hawaii Press. Copyright © 1969 by University of Hawaii Press. **Barbara Unger**, p. 185. "Breasts" by Barbara Unger is reprinted from *Wisconsin Review*, vol. 9, no. 3 (1973). **Louis Untermeyer**, p. 45. "Rapunzel" by Louis Untermeyer is reprinted from *The New Adam*, published by Harcourt, Brace and Howe in 1920. **Evelyn M. Watson**, p. 123. "A Sleeping Beauty" by Evelyn M. Watson from *Symbols of Immortality* used by permission of Christopher Publishing House. **Edith Weaver**, p. 76. "Lost Cinderella" by Edith Weaver is reprinted from *Poetry*, vol. 70, no. 2 (1947). **Gail White**, p. 19. "Happy Endings" by Gail White is reprinted from *Poem*, no. 34 (1978). **Elinor Wylie**, p. 122. "Sleeping Beauty" by Elinor Wylie from *Collected Poems of Elinor Wylie* used by permission of Alfred A. Knopf, Inc. Copyright © 1932 by Alfred A. Knopf, Inc. and renewed 1960 by Edwina C. Rubenstein. **Vitomil Zupan**, p. 108. "A Fairy Tale" by Vitomil Zupan is reprinted from *The Literary Review*, vol. 14, no. 3 (1971).

All illustrations in this book are from Hans Rühl (ed.), *Scherenschnitte von Luise Duttenhofer [1779–1829]: Faksimile-Druck von 147 Tafeln aus der Sammlung im Schiller-Nationalmuseum, Deutschen Literaturarchiv in Marbach*, published by A. T. Verlag (Aarau and Stuttgart). Copyright © 1978.